"What did we miss?" Addie asked, scanning the baseball field.

But there was no action down there; glancing up at the video board, Giff realized that the crowd's cheer had been in response to action on the KissCam. The televised image changed, and Giff stared, slow to process that he was looking at *himself*. Well, himself, plus two snoozing children and Addie, who was so close her head was nearly on his shoulder.

We look like a family.

Acting on impulse, he turned, lifting Addie's chin with his free hand. "We have to," he said with an unapologetic smile. "KissCam's an American tradition. Please," Giff added mischievously, "there could be a giant pretzel in it for you."

Addie pursed her lips. "I'm not that easy."

"I didn't think so." His mouth curved into a half smile. "But a man can dream."

Dear Reader,

In my June 2010 Harlequin American Romance, *The Best Man in Texas*, I introduced Giff Baker—one extremely attractive Houston businessman. After the heroine of that book decided not to marry him, however, I knew Giff deserved his own story and another chance at love!

Meet Addie Caine, single woman and newly appointed guardian to her orphaned nephew and infant niece.

When freelance consultant Giff is hired as Addie's project manager, she quickly learns that he is as kind and charming as he is good-looking. There's a lot about him to tempt a woman, but as she struggles to ace her crash course in parenting, she has little time or emotional energy left over for romance. Then again, Giff has already won over her six-year-old nephew and is great with the baby....

I am a strong believer in happy endings, both in books and real life, and I hope you enjoy watching these two people who have both suffered loss in their pasts work their way toward a well-deserved happy ending!

Best wishes,

Tanya

Texas Baby
TANYA MICHAELS

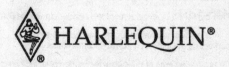

HARLEQUIN®

TORONTO • NEW YORK • LONDON
AMSTERDAM • PARIS • SYDNEY • HAMBURG
STOCKHOLM • ATHENS • TOKYO • MILAN • MADRID
PRAGUE • WARSAW • BUDAPEST • AUCKLAND

Recycling programs
for this product may
not exist in your area.

ISBN-13: 978-0-373-75325-3

TEXAS BABY

Copyright © 2010 by Tanya Michna.

ABOUT THE AUTHOR

Tanya Michaels began telling stories almost as soon as she could talk...and started stealing her mom's Harlequin romances less than a decade later. In 2003, Tanya was thrilled to have her first book, a romantic comedy, published by Harlequin Books. Since then, Tanya has sold more than twenty books and is a two-time recipient of the Booksellers' Best Award as well as a finalist for a Holt Medallion, National Readers' Choice Award and Romance Writers of America's prestigious RITA® Award. Tanya lives in Georgia with her husband, two children and an unpredictable cat, but you can visit Tanya online at www.tanyamichaels.com.

Books by Tanya Michaels

HARLEQUIN AMERICAN ROMANCE

HARLEQUIN TEMPTATION

*4 Seasons in Mistletoe

This story about building a family
is dedicated to the Michnas—
I couldn't have found a better family to marry into!—
with a special shout out to my brother-in-law.
No, I am not going to write a book about you,
but yes, you are hero material.

Also, go Astros!

Chapter One

The situation called for "cheerful" and "soothing." *Sorry, fresh out. But we are running a special on "desperate" and "borderline hysterical."*

It was well past midnight, and Addie Caine's nerves were shot. She'd tried patiently explaining this to her niece, but as it turned out, five-and-a-half-month-olds weren't open to reason. Or bribes. Of course, Nicole was shrieking too loudly to have heard anything her aunt offered.

"Please, please, *please* stop crying," Addie murmured as she paced her cluttered bedroom with the infant. Addie glanced at the door she'd closed in an attempt to keep the sound from carrying down the hall—which was probably as effective as trying to ward off a missile with a parasol. "I finally got your brother back to sleep, and you're going to wake him again."

Addie had never for a minute believed that parenting was easy. She just hadn't expected it to be *this* hard. Then again, as a twenty-eight-year-old single woman, she hadn't expected to become the instant parent of two, either.

Exhausted, Addie sank to the edge of her mattress,

misjudging the distance and narrowly missing the wooden finial of her pine and copper four-poster bed. She was too worn down to keep blocking the memories she'd tried to keep at bay, and the overpowering sense of loss that washed over her was far more painful than Nicole's skull-splitting wails. Addie's chest tightened at the memory of her brother's smile, the same smile her six-year-old nephew, Tanner, had inherited, although she'd barely caught a glimpse of it in the past month. Tanner's big brown eyes were far too solemn for a child who had previously been known to crash through the house attacking imaginary foes with a lightsaber.

He'd lost his suburban house in Corpus Christi the same weekend he'd lost his parents. He'd been uprooted to living with his aunt in a two-bedroom Houston apartment, starting first grade in a brand-new school where he didn't know anyone. Class had begun last week and his teacher, Ms. Phipps, reported that he hardly spoke. *He deserves so much more than this.*

Instead of his custom-painted playroom and big, fenced backyard, Addie had put him in her far-too-feminine guest room and had tried to convert her tiny home office into a nursery for Nicole. Once the Corpus house sold, she would use that money to buy a home here, something more kid friendly. But the market was slow right now and the listing was only a couple of weeks old.

Addie squeezed her eyes shut, but tears still leaked from the corners. It had been three weeks since she'd lost her big brother and his beautiful wife in a boating accident. They'd been so excited about the overnight excursion to the time-share beach house, their first away trip since Nicole had been born. Addie had gone down to stay with the kids and remembered her sister-in-law explaining to her how to prepare the bottles. "It took some effort," Diane had teased, "but she should have plenty of breast milk until I get back."

Three weeks later, Nicole had yet to adjust. She seemed perpetually ticked off about the formula Addie bought. Though it had been highly recommended by their new, Houston-based pediatrician, Nicole clearly deemed it inferior. *Sorry, kid, there's only so much I can do.*

Addie felt moments from giving up and just sobbing along with the baby. She forced herself to her feet, rocking and swaying her niece. Should she take Nicole to the front of the apartment, where the battery-operated swing was located? *My neighbors would kill me.* Addie's living room bordered the next apartment's master bedroom. She made a mental note for tomorrow: rearrange the jumble of boxed children's items and displaced office furniture now housed in her room to make a place for the swing. What she wouldn't give to have someone else here who could drag it back for her now, or someone just to offer moral support, for that matter.

If it weren't midnight, she might call her parents at their retirement community in Miami. Her mother had wanted to stay longer after the funeral to help, but Catherine and Edward Caine were both nearing seventy. There was a limit to how much they could physically do. Addie's best friend since college, Jonna Wilder, had a hot date tonight—an Astros home game followed by a late dinner with her new boyfriend. If things had gone as well as Jonna had anticipated, she probably wasn't home.

A month ago, Addie would have assumed she could call Christian for help. After all, she'd been planning to marry him, which implied some dependability in the whole "for better or worse" department. But her fiancé had fled for the hills some time between the reading of the will and baby Nicole yarfing down the front of his Brooks Brothers suit.

"Please understand, this doesn't mean I don't care about you, Addie. I just...I'm not ready for an instant family."

Yeah, well, neither was she, but what choice did she have? She owed these kids her best. Unfortunately, she felt like her best was woefully inadequate.

I need help. Nicole's face scrunched up into a nearly purple scowl and she let loose a shriek forceful enough that Addie expected her ceiling fan to crash to the floor.

Correction. I need a miracle.

THROUGH THE CELL PHONE's hands-free earpiece, a man whose voice was thick with Texas drawled, "Really appreciate your doing me this favor, Giff."

Giff Baker stared out his windshield, absently monitoring the Houston gridlock. The increased congestion was due in part to schools being back in session, but the sweltering heat still felt more like summer than early September. Other people might suffer from impatience or road rage, but Giff was too accustomed to the traffic to muster genuine irritation. "With the salary you quoted me, Bill, I'm not sure this qualifies as a 'favor.'"

Money aside, Giff was secretly grateful for the distraction of this unique, short-term job. It might keep him from dwelling on recently changed circumstances and his resulting... What, melancholy? A stupid word that made him sound like the brooding hero of a bad gothic piece.

Numbness.

Giff might pride himself on staying calm in the face of bumper-to-bumper traffic, but the truth was, it had been a while since he'd felt *any* strong emotions. At least Bill Daughtrie's offer left him genuinely curious. Giff was an IT consultant. With the exception of a few repeat clients, most of his jobs were short-term. He'd done work on network security, but this was the first time anyone had sought his services specifically as a corporate spy. *I'll be like James Bond.* But without the underwater jet-pack or grenade pen.

Bill Daughtrie was a fellow Texas A&M graduate who owned a relatively small but reputable civil engineering firm. He was determined to protect his company from the apparent traitor in his employ who was sharing—presumably, selling—key data with Bill's biggest competitor.

"Your timing couldn't be better," Giff said. "My schedule is abnormally light." He'd deliberately cleared it because he was supposed to have been married by now. They would have been back from their honeymoon, settling in as a couple.

For a moment, his fingers clenched around the steering wheel. He wasn't mad at Brooke—she certainly hadn't intended to fall in love with Giff's best friend—but Giff had enjoyed such a clear picture of where he thought his life was going, where he thought he wanted to be. Now, he felt directionless.

Alone, you mean. His best friend and ex-fiancée were in Hawaii, where they'd eloped, and Giff's only family, the mother he'd helped take care of while she fought breast cancer, had recovered with flying colors. She was on a singles' cruise to the Caribbean and planned to stay with old friends in Florida on the way back. The people who meant the most to him in the world were off in tropical locations and Giff was here. Stuck in traffic.

As he and Bill made plans to meet next Tuesday, Giff tried to sound professional about taking this job rather than absurdly eager. He had no idea what he'd find working undercover as a project manager in Bill's company, but one thing was abundantly clear: *I need a change.*

Chapter Two

"Girl, you look like hell."

Addie resisted smacking her coworker upside the head. *Probably because it would require lifting my arm and I don't have that kind of energy.*

"Tough night," she told Gabrielle Lopez, assistant to the marketing director. "Followed by a tough morning."

Whereas Gabrielle had probably been at the office for half an hour, Addie hadn't even made it to her desk. She'd made a beeline straight for the break room and the caffeine therein. Addie and the kids had survived Labor Day weekend at home—Nicole might even have slept for two consecutive hours on Saturday—but after a three-day holiday away from school, Tanner had been even more resistant to going back. She'd had to pry him off her and she'd felt horrible putting him on the bus. Intellectually, she knew it was for his own good and that she was simply making him join his peers for another day of educational enrichment. Emotionally, she'd felt as if she were making him walk the plank into shark-infested waters.

The ocean analogy reminded her abruptly of Zach

and Diane's accident, and her stomach muscles clenched as if she might be sick. *I miss him so much.* She could barely begin to imagine how awful it was for Tanner.

"It gets easier," Gabrielle was saying. "For the first year after the twins were born, I thought I was going to lose my mind."

"Thanks." Addie appreciated the sentiment and bit back the reminder that Gabrielle had the assistance of her husband and a huge extended family, most of whom lived just around the corner in League City. "I'm sure it will get better. Eventually. For now, I just need a seriously strong cup of coffee and I'll be fine." Or at least, less noticeably *not* fine.

Gabrielle grimaced, then said apologetically. "I just poured the last cup of the caffeinated stuff. But I've already got a new pot brewing," she added, pointing behind her.

Addie turned and watched fresh coffee drip far too slowly into the glass carafe.

"Caine, shake a leg!" From the doorway, Pepper Harrington—annoyingly impeccable in a tailored pantsuit and killer shoes—barked orders as if she outranked Addie in the office hierarchy.

Actually, they had both been hired about the same time. Addie often felt Pepper had zeroed in on her as a direct competitor because they were the only two women in the male-dominated IT department. Addie would have preferred to work more closely with Pepper and make them both look good, hopefully paving the way for more female IT employees in the future. But she had enough to worry about right now without sparing mental energy for Pepper's petty office politics.

"You're going to be late to the meeting," Pepper warned.

"On implementation strategies?" Addie frowned, trying to make her sleep-deprived brain function. "That's not until noon."

"They moved it to eight-thirty. Honest to God, do you even read your e-mails anymore? They're doing the strategy meeting this morning so that they can introduce the new project manager at noon." She smiled, oozing insincerity from her flawless pores. "You should rebutton your blouse between now and then. I'd hate for you to make a bad first impression."

Then she was gone, leaving the wicked witch's theme music stuck in Addie's head.

"That woman's heart is as black as her hair," Gabrielle mumbled.

Pepper had sleek, raven locks that fell halfway down her back—not unlike Gabrielle's silky, but shorter, dark hair. Addie, on the other hand, had coppery shoulder-length hair that curled uncontrollably whenever it was humid. Which, given that she lived in Houston, was pretty much every day. Some mornings she was able to do damage control with a curling iron, making the corkscrews at least look as if they were on purpose. Today, she'd settled on the less effective but far quicker solution of a barrette while also making Tanner's lunch and packing Nicole's bag. The baby attended a small, exclusive day care that cost more than Addie's monthly car payment.

"Pepper may not win any congeniality awards, but she's right. I can't walk around the office like this. I look like an idiot who can't dress myself." The closest ladies' room was one floor down and apparently Addie had a meeting she wasn't fully prepared for in—she glanced at the clock—two minutes. "Can you cover me?"

Gabrielle nodded, moving to the front of the room and blocking the doorway while Addie faced the back wall and hastily rebuttoned.

"Thank you."

"Good luck," Gabrielle said over her shoulder.

Once Gabrielle was gone, Addie stopped to marvel at the sensation of being alone. Moments of solitude that she'd once taken for granted were now a novelty. *It's so quiet in here.* No sound but the rhythmic burble and drip of coffee percolating. If she sat down, she'd be asleep in seconds.

Instead she pulled a compact out of her purse, scowling at the miniature reflection of her face. In her rush, she'd completely forgotten lipstick, she'd smeared mascara under one of her bloodshot, puffy eyes, and far from taming the red-gold frizz around her face, it seemed she'd merely angered it.

With a snarl, she unclasped the useless barrette in her hair, gave her head a brisk shake and reached for a cup. If she had to wait any longer for caffeine to hit her bloodstream, she was going to turn feral and start spooning ground beans directly into her mouth. As she poured, a few more drops fell and sizzled on the metal plate beneath, but the pot had mostly finished brewing.

Trying to walk and sip from a full coffee cup at the same time, she sloshed the hot liquid across her hand. When she jerked reflexively from the pain, more coffee splattered across the front of her blouse and she dropped the cup.

"Damn it!"

"Uh…anything I can do to help?"

Addie's gaze was blurred from lack of sleep and the cross-eyed agony of scalding herself. So it was possible that the man who'd just entered the break room was not gorgeous to an inhuman degree. But he sure looked it. He was tall, but not so much that she'd feel awkward next to him, with light brown hair. The gold highlights looked natural rather than salon-purchased. His features were handsome enough that he could have been leading man material at the box office.

That good-looking face was currently blank of all emotion as he studied her. She had a horrible flash of how *she* must look to *him,* standing there, hair on end, makeup ineptly applied, coffee staining her blouse. *On the upside, at least it's buttoned correctly.*

Addie wanted to laugh, but the sound that came out was more like a croak. Another followed and she realized she wasn't laughing at all. Just the opposite. The dam had finally cracked. Since getting the news that her brother and sister-in-law had died, she hadn't been able to fall apart. There had been the kids to think of and her parents to console, funeral arrangements to make, a house to sell, a storage facility to rent… At another time in her life, maybe her lover of three years dumping her might have warranted a good cry, but she'd pushed aside her anger with Christian the same way she'd repressed the grief for her brother. And now it all seemed to be welling up within her at once.

"Ex-excuse me." Not sparing the handsome stranger

another glance, Addie did what she'd secretly been wanting to do ever since the call from the Coast Guard. She fled.

"OH, HONEY." JONNA WILDER'S voice on the other end of the cell phone was two parts sympathy and one part self-flagellation. "I knew you were having a hard time, but I guess I've been so wrapped up in Sean…. You know what it's like in that first blush of love when you can't get enough of each other?"

Not really. Blowing her nose with the toilet paper she'd pulled from the dispenser, Addie tried to remember if it had been like that with Christian in the beginning. Maybe? She dimly recalled that he'd been a good kisser—nice technique—but in the past year they hadn't kissed much. Their sporadic love life had dwindled to bing-bang-boom, more habit than passion.

Even though she still thought it was callous timing to ditch a girlfriend when her life was in the midst of upheaval, she was starting to grasp that he'd probably done her a favor in the long run.

"You're entitled to have a life," Addie assured her friend. "Plus you get full credit for answering your phone this morning and talking me off the ledge." Metaphorically speaking. She wasn't even sure the windows in her seventh-story office opened. Instead, she'd escaped to the ladies' room which had remained mercifully empty for the ten minutes during which she'd cried so hard she thought she might throw up and then dialed Jonna's cell. Her friend worked in the administrative offices of an art museum and was still making her morning commute.

Aside from the fact that Addie could just imagine

Pepper smirking her way through the implementation meeting Addie was currently missing, she felt surprisingly better. More centered. Emptier, but in a good way, as though she was no longer carrying around a ticking bomb.

"Glad I could help," Jonna said. "I should probably be doing more, but I have less experience with kids than you do." She was the oldest of three unmarried sisters, none of whom had children.

"Don't worry about it. They're my responsibility and I'll figure out something. I just need a way to…connect with them more." She might not be able to chat with Nicole about current movies and politics—well, she could, it would just be a one-sided conversation—but Tanner was old enough to have established interests. As a kindergartener, he'd played both autumn and spring soccer last year. Was it too late to sign him up for a league this fall?

"Let's all have dinner some time this week," Jonna suggested. "Tomorrow night work for you? My treat. Not one of our usual places."

They tended to meet at Michelangelo's on Westheimer for special occasions like birthdays or promotions and one of the nearby La Madeleine cafés for quicker lunches and dinners.

"What did you have in mind?" Addie asked.

"One of those obnoxious pizza restaurants with kiddie rides and video games and employees costumed as large furry animal characters."

Addie thought about the potential noise level and seizure-inducing flashing lights. Then she thought about the possibility of seeing Tanner laugh. "You'd willingly spend an evening in a place like that?"

"That's how much I love you, babe."

"You are a true friend. Now that you've helped me regroup, I should get back to work." And probably poke her head into the break room to make sure there wasn't a puddle of coffee on the floor. With the way her luck was running, someone would slip and sue her butt.

Would the golden-haired stranger still be there?

She was relieved to discover that no, he was gone.

Thank God. It was not in Addie's nature to self-destruct like she had and knowing he'd witnessed it made her feel uncomfortably vulnerable. She'd prefer never having to face him again.

BEHIND THE MASSIVE MAHOGANY desk sat a suitably massive man. Bill Daughtrie was over six foot three and so broad-shouldered that his suits were probably custom-made. He'd been working on his MBA while Giff was an undergrad, and his thick, wavy hair had turned prematurely white in the past few years.

"As far as anyone here knows," Bill Daughtrie said, "you're contracted to be with our IT department for a few months, running the network forensics project. But I'd prefer to have this matter settled in the next three to four weeks. If I'm still losing bids three months from now…"

"I understand." Giff's usual creed was to stick with a job until it was completed to the client's satisfaction, but if he hadn't found anything within a month, it was unlikely he was going to find anything at all. And while he had some downtime in his professional schedule right now and flexibility in being self-employed, he couldn't juggle this with his other jobs indefinitely.

Bill had explained that he'd lost four major projects in the past year all to the same rival, even when he'd deliberately altered his bidding formula on the last one, cutting deeper into potential profits than he ever had before. The would-be client had later confessed that, in the current economy, he couldn't afford *not* to choose the lower bidder, but that he wanted Bill to know it had been a close choice between the two. Suspiciously close.

"I don't mind healthy competition," Bill added with a scowl, "but this is dirty pool and I have no intention of going down without a fight. Since you're the new guy, you can look at employees more closely than I can, under the guise of 'getting to know' them. Once you've compiled any findings for me, the legal team and I will take it from there. Hard evidence is, naturally, my dream scenario, but we'll start with just noting bizarre behavior."

Giff flashed to the redhead he hadn't quite met that morning. Did screaming an expletive and running from the room qualify as bizarre?

It did in his world.

His mother, his only family since his father died, was a woman who possessed a lot of poise and quiet strength. In her fight against cancer, she'd shown amazing courage. Giff's ex-fiancée, Brooke, had been cut from a similarly stoic cloth. Raised in a family of drama queens, Brooke had set herself apart by measured, rational actions. Meeting—and subsequently falling for—Jake McBride, Giff's childhood best friend, had cracked her composure, but it was still difficult for Giff to imagine Brooke in the same state as that poor woman today.

She'd been a mess.

And Giff was so unused to that kind of display, he'd had no idea how to react. For the few seconds they'd been in each other's company, he'd mostly stared, nonplussed. After her startling exit, he'd thrown away her dropped cup and cleaned up the coffee on the tile floor. Then he'd reported to Bill, who'd given him a tour of the offices before this final one-on-one briefing. Bill was catering an early lunch of sandwiches and chips in the large conference room so that Giff could start meeting people, then he was expected to sit down with his "team" at noon.

"I'm more experienced getting information from computers than people," Giff reminded him. He'd already asked Bill for the security clearance to do a network audit of object access. "But I'll try my best on both fronts."

"I know I can count on you," Bill said approvingly. "After all, you know what it's like to be betrayed."

Giff arched an eyebrow. "I'm self-employed. I don't quite follow the comparison."

"I wasn't talking about business, son."

Giff was mildly amused by the epithet that he knew to be more regional than literal. The other man couldn't be more than five years older.

"Your engagement," Bill elaborated. "Heard about it. Can't believe that gal, to say nothing of your—"

"Don't believe everything you hear," Giff said with a tight smile. "Brooke and I parted ways amicably. I wish her and Jake all the best." It should have occurred to Giff that gossip would run rampant. Houston might be the fourth largest city in the country, but his mother was a socialite and he was active in Houston's business community. People talked—they just did it through text messages instead of over backyard fences.

Not that it was any of "people's" business, but Jake McBride himself had helped Giff see that proposing to Brooke had been as much a knee-jerk reaction to his mother's illness as it had been to affection for Brooke. Oh, Giff was entirely fond of her, but it hadn't been deep and abiding love he'd felt.

Am I even capable of that? As an only child of two devoted parents, he'd had a front row seat to what real-life romance could look like. Of course, he'd also seen it ripped apart when his father died. Giff thought that, in the abstract, he wanted what his parents had shared. But maybe he didn't have the kind of courage required to take that risk because aside from in-the-moment desire, the most he ever seemed to feel for his girlfriends was vague warmth.

Maybe I'm the emotional equivalent of beige. A depressing notion.

Then again… He recalled the red-haired woman with the trembling hands who'd looked to be in the throes of some sort of emotional meltdown. *I'll take beige and dignified over* that *any day.*

Chapter Three

Even though the lunch spread was pretty pedestrian, mostly turkey on rye from a nearby deli, Addie grew ravenous at the sight of the food. Apparently, crying your eyes out worked up an appetite. She felt as if she hadn't been hungry in weeks and the sudden rumble in her stomach was a welcome change.

I'm back! After her embarrassingly late arrival to the morning meeting, she'd been able to contribute some good points that had had her coworkers nodding in agreement. Then she'd called to find out that, yes, the local soccer league *was* still taking applicants through the end of the week. The woman on the phone had said, however, that they'd been having a problem drumming up enough parent volunteers to coach.

"Experience isn't necessary," she'd stipulated. "This isn't a supercompetitive league where we play with referees and scoreboards. The emphasis is on the kids getting exercise, learning the fundamentals of the game and having fun."

On impulse, Addie had agreed to coach. After all, hadn't she been looking for a way to bond with her nephew? This was more doable than Plan B, taking her nephew on an intergalactic trek to find Yoda so they could train as Jedis together.

Only a few hours after her panicked phone call to Jonna, Addie had managed to regroup professionally and personally. Now she planned to chow down and meet the new project manager, dazzling him with her team spirit and helpful input.

Reaching for one of the deli's signature pickle spears, Addie became aware of an increased buzz in the conversation around her. Bill Daughtrie's name was mentioned. As much as he traveled and as busy as he stayed, even when in Houston, he didn't come to every meeting, especially not to introduce a contract worker who'd be gone before the holidays.

Telling herself that it wasn't eavesdropping if people were going to have their private conversations a foot away from her, Addie listened to Robert Jenner express exactly what she'd just been thinking.

"So either Daughtrie thinks there's something important about him or about this particular network project. What do we know about the guy?"

"They're both A&M alumni," Pepper answered. "And 'the guy' is Giff Baker."

Addie recognized the name but was still trying to place it when Jenner asked, "Is that supposed to mean something to me?"

Pepper snorted. "It might if you ever opened the *Chronicle* to anything but the sports page. Baker's from a wealthy family, has a longstanding relationship with several local charities, was supposed to get married this summer but the wedding was called off, and he's credited as having something of a Midas touch, doing some very successful consult work with dozens of corporations throughout the state."

Although Addie should only be concerned with his business achievements, since he would temporarily be the person she reported to at work, the wedding part snagged her attention. So he, like Addie, had been engaged? It sounded as if he'd been a lot further along in the process and she found herself wondering idly if he'd been jilted or if he'd been the one, as Christian had, to walk away.

"Good morning!" Bill Daughtrie entered the room with a booming greeting. Bill was the type of man who frequently boomed. "I see most of you have already started to dig in—please, keep eating. I just wanted your attention for a moment. To introduce Gifford Baker, who has agreed to temporarily act as a project manager in IT. Some of you are probably already familiar with Giff's record of excellence…"

The rest of Daughtrie's words were drowned out by the buzzing in Addie's ears when she noticed the tall man at the CEO's side. It was the hot guy from this morning.

Oh, hell.

Even though she hadn't said the words aloud, the hot g—her new boss suddenly turned to her, brows raised over his green eyes, as if he'd heard exactly what she was thinking.

GIFF WASN'T THAT SURPRISED to see the volatile redhead again. After all, he'd deduced from her presence in the break room that she probably worked here. But *she* certainly looked stunned to see *him*. After her first wide-eyed reaction, she'd ducked her head immediately to her plate of food. Yet even as Giff was shaking hands with the people Bill introduced, he was aware of the woman's gaze furtively returning to him.

Whenever he entered a company's environment, he went out of his way to put people at ease. Mostly, people were happy to have his expertise, but occasionally they were more territorial. He'd won over plenty of temporary coworkers who hadn't been initially welcoming. Should he go speak to her?

On the other hand, the last time he'd talked to her, she'd bolted from the room, so maybe he should let her finish her sandwich in peace.

As it turned out, he needn't have worried about the right tactical approach to take. She approached him. Giff was in the midst of conversation with Bill and a dark-eyed woman named Pepper when he sensed the redhead close to him. She cleared her throat delicately.

"Ah, Addie Caine," Bill said. "The other invaluable lady on our IT team. Addie, meet Giff Baker."

Automatically, Giff stuck out his hand. Looking reluctant but not having any gracious alternative, she took it. He didn't think the jolt that went through him was from the benign contact of their fingers. Instead, as her gray eyes locked with his, he was jolted by another type of contact altogether. He found himself searching those eyes for any trace of this morning's tears and felt seized by the unlikely urge to wipe them away. Her expression was determined, as was the tilt of her chin. What had made such a determined, and by Bill's accounts, capable woman seem so…broken this morning?

"Mr. Baker." Her voice was rich and husky. "Pleased

to meet you. I wondered if—I apologize if this is rude—I might steal a second of your time?"

There was no way he'd deny his curiosity by telling her no. "If you'll excuse me a moment, Bill?"

"Naturally." Bill let loose one of his hearty laughs. "After all, I'm the one paying for the grub and I haven't had a chance to eat any of it yet."

Only half-aware that Pepper was glaring her displeasure at the way this woman had swooped in to monopolize his time, Giff followed Addie to an empty corner on the far side of the room.

He kept his voice low. "So you're Addie."

"You were probably expecting something like 'Sybil.' Or 'Ophelia.' She was pretty loony there at the end," Addie muttered to herself. "Mr. Baker, you caught me at a bad moment this morning. And I want you to know, that never happens. Ever. Which leaves me with no experience in putting it gracefully behind me. I'm not asking for any kind of preferential treatment, I just… Is it possible for you to evaluate me on the same merits as everyone else on the team, as if you'd never seen me before? I promise I'll prove myself. I'm a consummate professional."

She sounded matter-of-fact and not boastful in her sincerity. Unlike that Pepper woman who'd somehow managed to rattle off her résumé highlights twenty seconds after their introduction.

"Of course," he agreed. "Clean slate going forward. Everyone's entitled to one bad moment, right?"

She exhaled a sigh of relief. "Thank you. You won't regret that decision. I really am—" She broke off, glancing down in surprise. Then she fished a phone out of her trousers' pocket. "Sorry. My phone was on vibrate. I have to take this. Addie Caine speaking."

The gentleman in Giff wanted to fade back into the crowd, giving her privacy for her conversation. But wasn't it Giff Baker, budding corporate spy's, job to snoop? So far, Addie was definitely the most erratic character he'd met. Besides, there was nothing stopping *her* from moving away if she didn't want him to overhear.

Instead, she stood rooted to the spot, her face paling. "He did *what?* Are you sure? No, I— Yes, of course. I understand. We—I'll be right there." With a decisive snap, she folded her cell phone in half and turned wide gray eyes on Giff. "I'm sorry, I can't stay for the meeting. I have to go."

She was already striding toward the door before he could ask for an explanation or find out how her ditching their first team meeting fit into the definition of *consummate professional.*

ADDIE SWERVED INTO A PARKING space. She'd driven to the elementary school on autopilot, tamping down all her emotions and thoughts in favor of concentrating on traffic and streetlights. Now that she was here, however, she noticed her hands had started to shake. *Tanner, in a fight?* She was absolutely horror-stricken by the idea.

Back when he'd been more playful, he could be over-exuberant at times. It wasn't unheard of for him to accidentally knock something over or run into someone because he'd been battling imaginary foes instead of watching where he was going. But he'd always been so sweet-natured, extra gentle and patient with the baby.

I've only had them three weeks. Surely I haven't screwed them up already?

Climbing out of the car, she sent up a silent prayer that she got better at this parenting stuff. Quickly. *Bro, if you're watching from on high, I could use some assistance.*

The smell of fish sticks wafting from the cafeteria hit her the minute she opened the front door. Down the hall, children passed in a line, herded by a teacher who continuously reminded them to "use walking feet" and keep their hands to themselves. Addie's mind flashed back to the principal's warning on the phone. *"We have a very clear policy, Ms. Caine, on suspending any student who lays hands on another child. When it comes to bullies and physical violence, we're a zero-tolerance school."*

Addie's stomach clenched. Would they really suspend a confused and hurt six-year-old? She almost groaned at the prospect of having to stay home with him. She'd already used a ton of personal days in the past couple of months, and she doubted that asking for more now would earn her points with the new project manager.

Rounding the corner, Addie walked into the main office, feeling just as guilty and self-conscious about being called in to see the principal as she imagined kids did. She cleared her throat tentatively to catch the attention of the woman filing behind the longer counter.

"Excuse me? I'm Addie Caine."

"Ah, yes." The woman slid her wire-rim glasses up onto her nose and regarded Addie through piercing blue eyes. "Tanner Caine's guardian, here to see Principal Willott."

The way she said "Tanner Caine" caused Addie's hackles to rise. She might as well have called him Miscreant Caine, and Addie wanted to shake the prim little woman. *Don't judge him, he's been dealt a blow that would devastate adults five times his age!* Since Addie didn't want to foster any misconceptions about violence running in their family, she kept her hands folded in front of her and nodded tightly.

"Right down this hall, first door on your left. They're expecting you."

Inside the principal's office sat not only Tanner and the principal but Heidi Lee, the school guidance counselor. Addie had met with the round-faced brunette the week before school started. Addie was gratified to see that the woman was sitting close to Tanner, her arm resting on the back of his chair in a friendly, almost protective manner.

"Ms. Caine." The principal's face was expressionless, but her voice sounded less stern than it had on the phone. "I applaud your getting here so quickly. It shows that you appreciate the gravity of the situation."

Sparing a brief nod to the woman behind the desk, Addie turned her full attention to her main concern—Tanner. "You okay, buddy?"

He squirmed, not meeting her gaze. "Sorry, Aunt Addie."

She swallowed, undone by the defeat in his tone.

"Tanner wasn't hurt in the altercation," Principal Willott said gently. "The other boy, however, had to see Nurse Connie."

"I didn't mean for him to fall!" Tanner squeaked, looking up then, his doe-brown eyes desperate. "I got so mad, and I know I shouldn't have pushed him, but I didn't mean for him... He was bleeding, Aunt Addie."

She winced on the other child's behalf.

Heidi Lee rose, one hand still on the back of Tanner's chair. "Tanner, I believe you're missing your lunch period. Why don't you come and eat in my office while the principal and your aunt talk?"

He cast Addie such a fearful glance that she wanted to gather him in her arms and refuse to let him out of her sight. Instead she told him, "That sounds like a good idea."

"But I'm not hungry."

"You shouldn't miss meals." The boy was already too scrawny. "Go with Ms. Lee. I'll be there in a few minutes." *I hope.* When she'd sped away from her office, Addie hadn't given much thought to how long she'd be gone. By the time she returned, Pepper would no doubt be campaigning for her termination.

The counselor led Tanner out and quietly shut the door behind them. Addie slumped into one of the vacated chairs.

"I'm so sorry," she said, sounding a bit like her nephew had. "He really is a good boy. Very sweet, wouldn't intentionally hurt a fly!"

"Yes, well. It won't be particularly easy to persuade the other boy's parents of that." Principal Willott leaned over her desk, steepling her chin on her fingers. "Ms. Caine, I realize that Tanner has just gone through a very tough time. It's unfortunate that the substitute teacher was unaware of the situation when she read the book about family to the class. But there are nearly eight hundred children in this school and dozens of them have gone through some sort of tragedy in the past year. I cannot accept that as an excuse for fighting."

"I understand," Addie said numbly.

"I believe Tanner when he says he didn't mean for the other child to fall into the art center, but Tanner never should have shoved him in the first place. The plain truth is that no student is going to make it through his school years without someone saying something upsetting to him, and striking out physically can never be the answer."

"I will talk to Tanner about that," Addie promised, glad to hear that the principal sounded at least empathetic and not like the woman up front who seemed prepared to label Tanner a bad seed at age six.

"According to our policy handbook, I have no choice but to give him some form of suspension," the principal said. "But, since we still have several hours left in the school day, here's what I can do. He'll go home with you, sentenced to one half-day suspension off the premises and, tomorrow, he can serve one day in-school suspension, doing his work in Ms. Lee's office.

"After that, he can return to his classroom with his peers—at which time, he'll need to apologize in front of the other kids to the boy he knocked down. And the teacher will see to it that the other boy apologizes for his insensitive remarks about Tanner no longer having parents."

"All right," Addie agreed. Not ideal, but it could have been worse.

"You'll impress on Tanner how important it is that nothing like this happens again?"

"Yes, ma'am."

"Good, then I'll let you go collect him and his things from Ms. Lee's office. I hope you'll take her up on her offer to provide whatever assistance she can. Please make appointments with her whenever necessary to discuss the transitions in Tanner's life. We want him to succeed, Ms. Caine, just not at the expense of our other students."

It was probably good advice. Addie could definitely use the help of a professional, although the thought of missing work to meet with the woman in the middle of the day made her cringe. Her employer had been fairly lenient about the two unexpected weeks she'd taken off when Zach died, but she got the sense that she was beginning to push her luck. Which begged the question…

Did she miss work for the rest of the afternoon to stay home with Tanner, or should she take him to the office with her?

Somehow, she doubted either solution would endear her to the new green-eyed boss.

Chapter Four

"You promise you'll be on your very best behavior?" Addie asked as she turned into the parking garage below her office building.

Tanner nodded, his gaze locked on his window. "Aunt Addie, can kids get suspended from other places besides school?"

Since she'd been busy trying to compose the world's most effective apology for Giff Baker, Addie didn't register the question at first. Even when she did a moment later, she wasn't sure what he'd meant by it. "What kind of other places?"

"Like if...if me or Nicole did something bad at home," he began, his voice tremulous.

"Oh, Tanner, no. I would never send you away. Not for one day, not even for a couple of hours. You are *stuck* with me," she said emphatically.

He finally met her eyes then, and she almost wished he hadn't. "Unless you die."

Oh, God. What now? Was she supposed to lie and tell the kid she was immortal?

Leaning across the parking brake, she hugged him from the driver's seat. It was awkward but heartfelt. "I love you. Hey, want to know what I did today?" She hoped she didn't sound as manic and desperate to change the subject as she felt. "I signed you up for a new soccer team."

"Soccer?" Was that a hint of enthusiasm she heard in his voice?

Hallelujah. "Yep! And I'm going to be your coach. Cool, huh?"

"Really?" He mulled this over before asking tentatively, "Are you good at soccer?"

"Sure am." It wasn't, strictly speaking, a dishonest answer. For all she knew, she might be *great* at soccer. She couldn't recall a specific instance of actually playing the game, but didn't all kids at some point? Maybe she'd turn out to be a natural. "But, uh, it's been a long time since I've been on a soccer field, so you may need to give me some pointers. Can you do that?"

His brown eyes were now positively shining. "Yes!"

Whatever else happened today—including the grim possibility of being asked to pack her desk—she knew she'd done at least one thing right. That call to the community soccer league had been a stroke of genius. *Not that I'll be able to pay his entry fee if I lose this job.*

"Come on, kiddo, Aunt Addie needs to get back to work if I'm gonna keep you in cleats and your sister in diapers."

Tanner reached for the door handle, wrinkling his nose. "She uses a lot of diapers."

"That she does," Addie agreed. But the number of diapers Nicole went through wasn't nearly as daunting as what the future held: potty training. Taking deep breaths, Addie reminded herself that was still years away and resolved not to think about it. She'd already had her meltdown for the day.

In the elevator, she rifled through Tanner's book bag to see if he had enough to keep himself entertained for the afternoon. A math worksheet and a *Ready, Freddy!* chapter book looked like they'd be a good start. Beyond that, he had a plastic case of art supplies. There was a collection box for scrap paper that would be recycled near Gabrielle's desk. Maybe Addie could snag some in case Tanner felt like coloring.

"This way," she murmured.

He looked at her funny. "Why are you whispering?"

She supposed she'd been subconsciously encouraging him to be quiet while he was here, which was ironic. Ever since he'd come to live with her, she'd worried about how silent and withdrawn he'd become. She'd repeatedly attempted to draw him out of his shell, hoping for flashes of his old, animated self.

"Does everyone hafta whisper here?" he asked.

"No." Just people who ducked out of important meetings and were trying to sneak a kid inconspicuously into the office. "Come meet my friend Gabrielle. You'll like her. If you're polite, I bet she'll give you a piece of candy."

The oversized candy bowl Gabrielle kept behind her desk was legendary. No generic peppermints, but instead premium candies and minisized chocolate bars. People from all departments found excuses to come talk to her, especially late in the day when they needed the sugar rush to help get them to five o'clock.

Gabrielle's "office" was actually a top-of-the-line cubicle that went from the floor to the ceiling. No windows, but there was a doorway in the partition. The woman's dark eyes widened when Addie poked her head inside.

"There you are! Where on earth have you been? I heard you went AWOL."

Addie sighed. "Minor emergency at Tanner's elementary school." She ushered the little boy in front of her. "He's, uh, going to hang out with me for a few hours."

Gabrielle's eyebrows shot up, disappearing beneath her bangs. But she smiled gamely at Tanner. "Glad to meet you. I'm Gabrielle Lopez. But you can call me Gabi. I don't suppose you like chocolate do you?"

His eyes brightened and he took an automatic step toward her before stopping, his shoulders slumped. "I love chocolate. But I'm sorta in trouble right now. I probably don't deserve any."

"Do you swear to me," Addie began, "that you will *never* shove another child, even ones who tease you about not having a mother or father?" She tried diligently not to think vindictive thoughts, such as children who would tease parentless orphans probably deserved a poke in the arm.

"I promise."

"Then it's okay with me if you have a candy bar," Addie told him.

Friendly sympathy laced Gabrielle's voice as she held up the flowered plastic bowl. "How 'bout you, Aunt Addie? You look like you could use a candy bar, too."

Truer words...

Licking chocolate from her fingers a few satisfied

minutes later, Addie felt comforted enough to face Giff Baker with her apologetic explanation.

But feeling ready didn't keep her from flinching when she nearly ran into him at the entrance of Gabrielle's cubicle. "I was just coming to find you," she blurted, resisting the impulse to shove Tanner further behind her.

Giff seemed skeptical. "What a coincidence. I guess it's lucky then that the marketing director asked me to come talk to Ms. Lopez about a software update." His gaze trailed downward, his bland expression giving way to surprise. "And who do we have here?"

"My nephew, Tanner Caine." She mentally crossed her fingers that Giff was the type who could be swayed by a cute kid. He'd been on the brink of marriage—was he an aspiring family man, or had he, like Christian, balked at the idea? "Tanner, this is my project manager, Mr. Baker."

"Addie, if you and Mr. Baker need to talk," Gabrielle piped up, "Tanner can keep me company. That is, if the software discussion can wait just a little bit?"

"Certainly," Giff agreed. "Ms. Caine? I'd like the opportunity to catch you up on what you missed in the IT meeting."

She followed him to a small meeting room where she sank into a chair as soon as possible, shaky from the day's events. Giff closed the door and remained standing, his arms folded across his broad chest. For a long, barbed moment he said nothing. Addie's stomach flipped—she needed job security more than ever, this was not the time to be screwing up at work—and she bit her lower lip to prevent nervous babbling. He was peering at her with such intense scrutiny that she squirmed in her seat, half expecting that he'd start firing questions at her. *Where were you on the night of August fourth?*

In contrast to her imagined interrogation, his tone was softly inquisitive. "I'm guessing Tanner is the reason you had to leave. Call from the school nurse?"

"School principal," she corrected. With some of the flu epidemics in recent years, she didn't want him to think she'd brought a sick child into the office. "He, uh, got into a bit of trouble this morning. You probably never got in trouble in school." The last was an overly familiar afterthought, not meant to be spoken aloud. He just looked so annoyingly *perfect,* gorgeous in his well-tailored suit, a touted golden boy in the business world.

She immediately wished she could take it back, but he didn't look offended by the observation. On a day where she'd fallen apart in the break room and bailed on a meeting, one throwaway comment probably didn't even register.

"Only trouble by association," Giff said, leaning on the edge of the table. "My best friend was a hothead. He had good intentions but didn't always think through the consequences."

The admission was disarmingly human. With his six-foot height and strong jaw, it was difficult to picture Giff as a little boy with a best friend, much less a hotheaded buddy who dragged him into scrapes.

"Tanner's a great kid, but he lost his parents this summer. He and his baby sister ended up with me as a guardian and it's been..." She trailed off, since saying it had been *hard* for her nephew seemed like such an inane understatement. "We're all still adjusting."

Giff's green eyes reflected a flash of surprisingly deep emotion. "I know what it's like to lose a parent," he said. "Although, I was fortunate to have my father for all of my childhood. He died when I was in college. I'm sorry for Tanner's—for your—loss. You said he was your nephew?"

She tried to swallow past the lump in her throat, nodding when she couldn't quite find her voice. "M-my brother and his wife died after their boat capsized. Both of my parents are alive and even though I've been reading books and talking to the counselor at Tanner's school, I just can't wrap my head around what he must be going through. What it's like for a little boy to be completely uprooted and—Nicole, who's five months, cries all the time and I don't have a clue what I'm doing, but I actually think she'll bounce back easier. She barely knew her parents. Tanner..."

While she was talking, Giff had come closer. Now he startled her by reaching out to gently squeeze her shoulder. It was a simple, innocuous touch, just a gesture of reassurance. But she'd felt so isolated lately, the person who'd been doling out comfort, not on the receiving end of it.

"Thank you," she breathed. "I didn't mean to get carried away like that. You've *really* caught me on a bad day," she concluded with a hoarse chuckle.

"The bad days will get fewer and farther between," he said. "Eventually."

She sniffed. "You're a nice man."

"Don't sound so surprised."

"I just meant... Considering what your impression of me must be, you're being nicer than I deserve." Odd, how a stranger was showing her more kindness than the man she'd been planning to marry. From the day Christian had realized she now came with two children to the day he'd left for good, he'd been increasingly cold and impatient.

Giff was no longer touching her—probably for the best, since they were in full view of anyone who walked by the windowed room—but he was just close enough that she could feel his warmth, breathe in the rich smell of expensive soap.

"Don't shortchange yourself, Ms. Caine. Your co-workers have a pretty high opinion of you, and that helps shape my impression. During the team meeting, several topics came up that led to people telling me that I should get *your* opinion."

Addie was flattered. And dutifully ignored the cynical voice in her head that said if Pepper had been one of those suggesting he get Addie's input, she was only doing so to highlight Addie's absence. "I really am sorry that I wasn't there. I can't stay late this evening, but maybe tomorrow—"

He held up a hand. "I trust that you can get up to speed without burning the midnight oil. Will Tanner return to school tomorrow?"

"Absolutely."

"Then I'll see you in the morning. For now, I need to speak with Ms. Lopez about those software changes." He turned toward the door but didn't actually move. "Is there anything else I can do for you in the meantime?"

It might have been a rhetorical question, one she

should graciously acknowledge without placing any actual demands on him. But he looked so sincerely willing to help.

"Just one thing," she said, speaking quickly before she could think better of asking more favors. "Tanner loves soccer, and I've enrolled him on a team that's about to start its fall season, hoping it will give him something normal and familiar to enjoy. But his age group was short a few coaches." She hesitated, her boldness faltering.

Giff's eyes were wide, his brow furrowed. "Um, football—the American version—was always more my game. I don't have any experience with soccer."

"What?" Addie blinked, and then let out a peal of laughter. "I wasn't asking *you* to coach. I already volunteered. I was just trying to work up the nerve to tell you that I might have to periodically duck out a few minutes early in order to make it to practices on time."

"Oh." He lowered his head, looking both relieved and embarrassed. "That makes more sense. And it shouldn't be a problem as long as your work doesn't suffer."

"It won't. Thank you so much for your understanding. Tanner loves sports, and I'm really hoping this will be a good way to connect with him."

"How's he feel about baseball?" Giff asked. "You know Bill Daughtrie's sponsoring that employee day at Minute Maid Park this weekend?"

She nodded. It was an annual event that had become tradition. "We're already planning to go."

"Great. Then I'll see you there." Giff shook his head, his smile self-deprecating. "In addition to seeing you at the office probably every day this week."

"I knew what you meant."

As far as she knew, the entire office and their families had been invited to the Astros home game. It was as far from an intimate setting as one could possibly get, so there was absolutely no reason for her to flush with pleasure at Giff's words. She did anyway.

Chapter Five

Addie was struck by the irony—at home, where Nicole was surrounded by soothing sounds, like her lullaby CD and a crib attachment that played calming white noise, the baby never slept. Here at Puck E. Pizzas, which matched Houston Hobby Airport's runways decibel for decibel, amidst the pinging video games, squealing children and a vivacious house band (made up of animatronics barnyard livestock), Nicole was cheerfully comatose. She was drooling on her pink bib, her dimpled arms and legs splayed in all different directions as she slept in her carrier.

Of course, Addie would probably pay for this later. No way would the infant girl sleep tonight, but it was almost worth the long hours ahead to have a few minutes of peace, allowing her to catch up with Jonna. *Another irony.* A month ago, Addie would have considered this overly loud, overly bright pizzeria the antithesis of "peace." She was adapting.

Two twin boys zoomed past the booth, arguing loudly about who got to use the last token. One of them nearly knocked Jonna's drink off the corner of the table. Jonna grimaced, the expression out of place on her. She was an irrepressibly bubbly blonde. Addie loved her friend's natural optimism but had marveled during their university roommate years that anyone could be so cheerful first thing in the morning without chemical assistance.

"I'll admit," Jonna began, "that falling for Sean has led to the occasional wedding daydream, but this place certainly cures me of any baby longing I felt. Oh, shoot. That was insensitive, wasn't it? You know I didn't mean anything against Tanner or Nicole."

Addie set down her diet soda. "It's okay. I don't blame you for not being ready for motherhood. Hell, *I'm* not ready." The statement caused just enough guilt that she immediately glanced upward, checking on Tanner, even though there was no way he could have heard her confession. He was in the same place he'd been when she looked two minutes ago and the few before that.

In addition to the kid-friendly arcade games and scaled down carnival-style rides, the pizzeria boasted a huge labyrinth of overhead tubes that ran the length of the ceiling. The entry stairs and exit slide were only a few feet away from Addie, but the maze also featured plenty of thick plastic windows so that anxious kids or mothers could easily spot each other. Tanner had scurried up inside the tubes and now seemed content to sit in his chosen spot watching all the action unfold beneath him. She wished he were interacting more with the other nine jillion kids here, but he was smiling, so who was she to judge?

"I can't believe how crowded it is on a Wednesday night," Addie said. At least half the children present were old enough that they'd have school tomorrow. She'd already cautioned Tanner that they couldn't stay too late;

tomorrow was his first day back in the classroom since the principal's call yesterday.

Instead of letting herself worry over whether Tanner would have any more trouble with his classmates, Addie glanced back to her friend. "You are a saint. Thank you so much for suggesting this. Nicole's out like a light, and Tanner seems genuinely excited to be here."

Jonna quirked her lips. "That's his 'excited'? Don't get me wrong, I'm glad he's better behaved than some of the little monsters who've crashed into me since we got here, but…"

"I know. Soccer starts next week. Maybe that will help him perk up. Hey," Addie protested as her friend tried to stifle a laugh. "Stop that. It's not funny."

When she'd discovered over their pepperoni pizza that Addie would be coaching the team, Jonna had dissolved into giggles.

"Sorry. I don't even know why I find it so amusing. It's just not how I picture you, wearing a cap and whistle, giving motivational pep talks to a bunch of first-graders. But I applaud your decision. It will be great for you and Tanner. And maybe even for your social life."

Addie rolled her eyes. "*What* social life?"

"Precisely my point. You haven't mentioned dating since that rat Christian left. Can I just say again how much better off you are without him? Now you're free to meet someone new."

There were all kinds of freedom. While it was true Addie was single again, she wasn't exactly unencumbered.

"Jonna, it's not like I'm sitting at home worrying about how to meet men. I've been a little busy." Sitting at home worrying about finding the best possible day cares, the proper temperature of rice cereal, whether letting a small boy watch a movie in which droids were dismembered would scar him for life, or at least cause nightmares...

"Maybe the right guy for you is someone with parenting experience," Jonna said, looking excited as she warmed to the idea. "A single dad who's just as busy, who can empathize with what you're going through, who might be coaching his own child's soccer team."

For a second, Addie allowed herself to buy in to her friend's fantasy. It would be nice not to feel so alone, to get someone else's input on when to obsess over something and when to shrug it off as merely a phase or normal childhood challenge. She tried to picture a kind-faced single father with a quick smile and shoulders broad enough to lean on. Instead, her mind conjured Giff—probably as a reminder that, after the kids, work should be her top priority right now, not romance.

She shook her head firmly. "Sorry. Next to Tanner, the only guy in my life is Giff Baker."

Jonna choked on her drink, spluttering. "*What?* How did you meet him?"

Addie was thrown by her friend's reaction. "I told you all about him. I'm working with him, at least for a couple of months."

"He's the project manager? You never specifically mentioned his name."

"I didn't realize his name would mean anything to you. Do you recognize it from local business news?"

"No, from his patronage of the arts. Our paths have crossed at a couple of charity benefits where I was representing the museum. You told me that the man you embarrassed yourself in front of was attractive, but, wow. I didn't realize you meant someone who looked like *that*."

With a groan, Addie covered her face, reliving her first meeting with Giff. The good news was she hadn't had any humiliating moments since Tuesday. But she didn't really think she'd done anything stellar enough to counteract Tuesday, either. Hence her determination to work hard and impress Giff. Though he wouldn't be her supervisor for very long, he reported directly to Bill Daughtrie. Not only did she desperately want to keep her job, Addie was hoping for a raise after her next employee evaluation.

Her grocery bill would only continue to go up once Nicole started eating real food. The expense of soccer was manageable, but the years to come might hold music lessons and summer camps. Braces, she thought, recalling many an afternoon when she'd been dragged along to her brother's orthodontist.

"Munchkin alert," Jonna said, angling her chin toward the red slide.

Tanner scrambled off the slide, then retrieved his sneakers from the open-faced plastic shoe locker. Addie was ready with a bright smile when he reached the table.

"Hey, buddy. Did you change your mind about taking me on in air hockey?"

"Maybe later," he said noncommittally. "I came down 'cause I was thirsty."

Addie handed him his soda and a couple of tokens

when he asked if he could play the pinball machine behind her.

"After that, I'll carry Nicole around and we'll see what's on the other side of the restaurant," she offered. "Okay?"

"Sure."

"And you remember what I said about not staying too late, right?"

He scrunched up his face, his tone long-suffering. "I remember."

Across the table, Jonna chuckled.

Sending her friend a sidelong look of reproach, Addie ruffled the boy's hair. "All right, then. Just wanted to make sure we were on the same page."

He scampered off before she could issue any other reminders.

"You might not feel like a natural at this," Jonna teased, "but that was definitely a 'yes, mother' moment. You must be doing something right."

"Thanks." Addie waited a beat so it would seem as if she was making casual conversation rather than bursting with curiosity. "So you've actually met Giff? Anything I should know about him, since I'm reporting to him at work?"

"That's the only reason you're asking?" Jonna knew her too well.

Addie shrugged. "I admit it, the guy's gorgeous. But I don't have any plans to seduce him in the conference room or anything. Even if I had time to date, it certainly wouldn't be with a coworker." Worse, one who was above her in the chain of command. She could just imagine the field day Pepper would have with that! Accusations of unprofessional conduct and favoritism—no pair of green eyes was worth that kind of trouble.

"I don't know much that would be pertinent to your working with him, but I know he was engaged as recently as a few months ago," Jonna said. "By the time I was introduced to him, he was dating her. Brooke something, she's a journalist, I think. They were actually a cute couple. I was shocked when I heard she'd left him."

"*She* left *him?* You're sure?" Addie wondered what had happened to make a woman throw over a guy like Giff—strikingly handsome, successful and, if his easy forgiveness was any indication, good-natured.

"Fell for some other guy, I think. Poor Giff, jilted and on the rebound." Jonna grinned unabashedly. "Too bad I'm with Sean now and unavailable to comfort him."

Addie laughed. "You're terrible."

"How set are you on this no coworkers policy?" Jonna asked. "Maybe the two of you could comfort each other! Your broken hearts give you something in common."

"Please. I'm not brokenhearted over Christian." It almost seemed disloyal, how little she'd missed him since he left. She searched for the right words to articulate her feelings. "I never thought he was like, my soul mate, the one man on the planet I was destined to be with. But I thought I could count on him, you know?"

"I know," Jonna commiserated. "But you're still better off without him. And I'd just like to point out, for the record, that Giff is only doing contract work."

"What does that have to do with anything?"

"You said you wouldn't date a coworker." Jonna smiled slyly. "Well, he won't be your coworker for long."

THOUGH METEOROLOGISTS AGREED that the high temperature would again be in the nineties today, the early morning breeze was just cool enough to make one believe fall might be around the corner. Bill Daughtrie had an eight o'clock tee time and was warming up at the club's driving range. He'd asked Giff to meet him here so that they could talk without anyone from the office interrupting.

"So…" Bill stepped up to the ball, pausing thoughtfully before he swung. "What are your thoughts so far?"

Giff chose his words carefully, aware that his opinions would affect the men and women he'd been working alongside this week. He liked them. Addie Caine particularly came to mind. Family had always been important to Giff—it was one of the reasons, he'd realized in retrospect, that he'd become hastily engaged—because he'd been so eager to build a family. He could identify with the pain of her recent loss and admired the way she was doing her one-woman best to provide a family for her niece and nephew.

"Obviously I don't have proof of anything yet," Giff said, "or I would have brought it to you immediately. But the very lack of a noticeable cyber trail may mean someone with IT access and knowledge is responsible."

Daughtrie had confided that after the first three bids were lost, he'd kept the last one confidential, taking the advice of his management team to lower the bid into consideration but not sharing with them the final numbers. Yet, if his suspicions were correct, someone had still managed not only to get that information but to pass it along to the competition. Most anyone could erase data, superficially, but they should have left electronic fingerprints, a trail Giff could start unearthing that would lead to the guilty party.

Bill straightened, his expression hard. "Someone from my IT department is trying to screw me over?"

"I hope to figure that out," Giff said, noting the flare of anger in the other man's eyes and hoping he wouldn't make any rash decisions. "Right now, it's a hunch. A logical one, but still a hunch."

"Then I guess I'd better let you get back to the office so you can find me more information. You probably want to pay special attention to those two women," Bill drawled, lining up his next shot.

Once again, Giff's thoughts zeroed in on Addie. "What do you mean?"

"They make less money. Than the men. I've seen that lead to a chip on the shoulder with women before." He said this impatiently, dismissively, and Giff couldn't help thinking how big a "chip" Bill would have if someone tried to undervalue *his* work. "Think resentment could lead to a motive?"

"If you gave them equitable pay," Giff snapped, "there'd be no reason for resentment."

Bill bristled. "Hey, I made both of them damn good offers, comparatively speaking. Women in IT simply don't earn the same as their male counterparts. You know that. Everyone knows that."

Giff ground his teeth together. It was bad business to

smack the person you worked for with a golf club. Bill spoke the truth, but that didn't make it right.

On the drive to the office, Giff thought about what Bill had said.

Giff was talented in the field of network security, finding possible weaknesses and addressing them. In fact, half of what Bill was paying him for was to evaluate and implement new security measures that could be put in place to prevent something like this from happening after Bill had caught the culprit. But although Giff had some experience halting cyber theft, he was hardly a detective. He didn't know what emotion would drive a person the hardest. Was simple greed alone enough to corrupt someone, or was Bill correct in thinking that it might be greed fueled by righteous anger? It would be easier to rationalize stealing from someone if you legitimately felt they owed you anyway.

But maybe it wasn't straightforward greed so much as desperation. Someone who had to cope with mounting medical bills or gambling debts. *Or two new members of the family?*

On some level, Giff had been preoccupied with Addie Caine all morning, but this was the first time thoughts of her left him cold. Just how long ago had she become the guardian, the person financially responsible, for her niece and nephew?

Don't be ridiculous. Addie didn't steal confidential information from Bill, much less sell it.

He recalled the moment he'd first seen her, so upset that her emotions were a palpable force in the room. Unused to such blatant displays of feeling, he'd been downright uncomfortable in her presence. He also considered the way she'd spoken to him about Tanner, her pride and affection for the little boy as nakedly visible as her concern that she might not know what was best for him. All of Giff's instincts screamed that a woman with her generously giving nature was incapable of theft. Even if she was frantic enough to try it, she was too easy to read. In the three days he'd known her, he'd witnessed how she wore her heart on her sleeve. Not one with a cool poker face, Addie Caine.

Then again, how well did he really know her? Giff had worried about Bill making snap decisions without hard evidence, but wasn't that what Giff was doing? Removing Addie from suspicion based on a gut feeling, based on the hope that she wouldn't do anything wrong?

That settled it then. He'd just have to get to know Addie better.

Chapter Six

Darn you, Jonna. Addie blamed her friend's comments about Giff last night for her own lack of concentration in today's meeting. *"He won't be your coworker for long."* Maybe not, but he was for right now, and Addie needed to focus on his message to the team, not notice that he looked even better than usual. He'd taken off his jacket, rolling the sleeves of his shirt up to reveal the corded muscle of his forearms. His hair, for once, wasn't cover model perfect. Not disheveled, but just windblown enough to be touchable, as if she could run her fingers through it without worrying that she'd knock a strand out of place.

None of which had anything to do with network security.

"Ms. Caine, Addie?" Giff had requested that everyone call him by his first name and was making an effort to reciprocate, but Addie got the impression that he was actually more comfortable being formal. It wasn't that he was cold by any stretch of the imagination, just that he— "Did I say something that confused you? You appear a bit lost."

"Maybe it's just because you've missed so many

meetings lately," Pepper interjected with faux concern, swiveling in her chair to smile back at Addie. "I'd be happy to have lunch with you, get you up to speed."

Robert Jenner, behind Addie, tittered. Others took sudden interest in the polished surface of the cherry-wood conference table. Addie wondered how defensive it would make her look if she reminded everyone that technically she'd only missed the one meeting this week. She'd just been substantially tardy to another.

"Actually," Giff said from the head of the oval table, "why don't you have lunch with me, Addie? I hope you don't mind, Pepper. It occurred to me that, as project leader, it's really my responsibility to make sure everyone on the team is clear about our objectives."

Addie was stunned—and a little embarrassed—by his invitation. It wasn't as if she needed to be tutored! Then again, she could hardly admit that the reason she'd seemed "lost" was that she'd been lusting after him. Besides, Pepper's annoyed expression was somewhat mollifying. The woman clearly regretted that her attempt to make Addie look bad had resulted in a lunch date.

Not "date," lunch meeting. *Appointment. Two-person seminar.*

"Lunch would be great," she heard herself say, willing Giff to drop the subject and move on to a topic other than her.

"Wonderful. Now, back to what we were discussing. Our upcoming tasks are not unlike when banks and big corporations hire people to break in, so that security vulnerabilities can be discovered and addressed. I'd love to hear all of your thoughts on how you'd breach the network and how you'd hide your tracks." He flashed a wicked smile. "You know how actors are always saying it's more fun to play the bad guy? Now's your chance to think like a criminal."

Addie cleared her throat, anxious to say something—anything—that made her sound engaged in the discussion and mentally alert. "Why stop at hiding tracks? I mean, with the right programmer, there's a good chance the trail would eventually be uncovered, so why not do something diversionary, make it look like someone else's tracks? Most people would stop there and not 'waste' time by bothering to look further."

"Interesting." Giff's eyes were narrowed on her in a way that reminded her of Tuesday afternoon, when she'd been alone with him in the smaller conference room and had thought, for a moment, that he would start interrogating her at any second.

But maybe she was projecting too much intensity where really there was just thoughtfulness.

After a moment's consideration, he inclined his head. "Go on. Please."

She'd mostly been thinking out loud, so she faltered, trying to come up with plausible explanations of what she'd meant. But her training and talent for her job kicked in and she found herself outlining a couple of loose possibilities. Even though it would take a lot of time, combined with trial and error, to evaluate the specifics of such a plan, her coworkers seemed suitably impressed.

Robert Jenner chuckled, this time not at her expense. "That's some serious food for thought, Caine. Who would have guessed that cute smile hid such a devious mind?"

"I'll say," Pepper agreed. She shot Addie a coolly assessing glance over her shoulder. "Remind me never to trust you."

GIFF'S GAZE STRAYED TO the time displayed at the bottom corner of the computer screen, leaving him unsure whether he should be amused or annoyed with himself. He and Addie had planned to meet in front of the elevators at noon. He still had a few minutes before then, and he'd been glancing at the clock with the eager frequency of a fourteen-year-old anticipating his first date.

Ironically, he wasn't sure he even *wanted* to take Addie to lunch. It had been an impulsive gesture, which was unlike him. Pepper's cattiness toward her co-worker had inspired a sudden, gallant protectiveness. *I wonder if this is how Jake usually feels about people.* Giff's best friend since childhood, Jake McBride, was hero material. Now a fireman who rescued people on a regular basis, Jake had first met—and rescued—Giff in the fourth grade. At the time, Giff had been cornered by three bullies intent on beating up the privileged kid. Having Jake on his side had evened up the fight.

The two men had grown up as close as brothers, but when Giff's fiancée had canceled their wedding because she'd fallen for Jake well, the dynamic had become more awkward between all of them. Giff wasn't truly angry; he'd given them his blessing. But he hadn't rushed to return Jake's phone message, left on Tuesday, that said he was back in town and wanted to get together.

One of their favorite places to meet was a small, family-owned Mexican restaurant, Comida Buena. Giff's mouth watered just thinking about it and he wished he could take Addie there, but the drive was too long. Reflexively, he checked the time again. Not quite twelve, but he might as well go since he wasn't getting any work done here.

On the one hand, Addie was a lovely, intelligent woman whom he genuinely liked. But that made considering her as a potential thief unpleasant. Equally discomfiting was Addie's candid personality. She was just so different from the other women he knew—his stoic mother, who'd faced losing her husband and battling a disease; some of the polished Houston socialites he'd dated; his habitually reserved former fiancée. Not being a demonstratively emotional person himself, Giff felt as if he were walking on eggshells around more expressive people. Jake had picked on him in college because Giff agonized over every romantic breakup, his biggest dread that a girl might cry and he wouldn't know what to do. One ex-girlfriend had even teased him about his innate aloofness.

"You sure you're from Texas?" she'd asked. "Lone Star boys wear jeans, drive trucks and sing country music when they get their hearts broke. I think you were supposed to be born British. Stiff upper lip and all."

Calm in the face of crisis made him a great consultant. Clients could pull him in to deal with seemingly overwhelming problems that he helped them solve. And right now, Bill Daughtrie was the paying client. Despite Giff's annoyance with the other man this morning, he fully intended to do his job and scrutinize the IT team.

Hardly a chore when the person under his scrutiny had soft hair that framed her face in beguiling copper curls and great legs beneath her short black skirt. Addie stood waiting in the marbled corridor, and his gaze slid down over her, undisciplined and appreciative. The first time he'd seen her, he hadn't realized how beautiful she truly was. Which was understandable, given that she'd been tear-stained at the time and had been flying past him.

Since there were only two women on his team, it was difficult not to notice the stark contrasts between them. Pepper was, objectively speaking, a very attractive woman. But with her very long hair, sharp features and designer suits, there was something almost aggressive about her good looks. Addie was more like a painting that drew the eye again and again, each time enticing the viewer to notice something new, to appreciate her more fully.

He forced himself to meet her eyes, hoping that none of that appreciation was evident on his face. "Addie. Thanks for meeting me. You in the mood for anything specific?"

She shook her head. "I'm not picky. But before we go... You don't really have to take me to lunch. It might look like I need the extra hand-holding, but—"

"I don't think that at all," he assured her. With every interaction they'd had this week, she'd proven herself an asset to the team and a quick thinker.

Had Jenner's joking words this morning been more

prophetic than he could know? Did Addie's bright mind hide a devious streak?

"But I'd really like to have lunch with you," he said.

"All right then." She flashed him a shy smile. "Anything but Puck E. Pizzas."

DESPITE THE OPPRESSIVELY muggy heat, they decided to walk to a nearby bistro. It hardly seemed worth the parking hassle just to go a few blocks.

"Besides," Addie admitted, "I need the exercise if I'm going to keep up with a bunch of kids on the soccer field. I'm supposed to get my team roster and a box of uniforms this weekend."

"For their sakes, I hope the weather cools down soon," Giff said. "When I look back on my athletic days, I wonder how the heck I did it. Jake and I had two-a-day football practices every summer when we were in high school."

"Jake?" she echoed, trying to remember if he'd mentioned that name before.

"The hotheaded childhood friend I told you about." Giff's smile was bittersweet. "I'm an only child, but he's like family."

Her thoughts veered toward her brother. Feeling a pang, she quickly turned her attention back to Giff. "So the two of you are still close?"

Giff stopped beneath the awning of the restaurant and held the door open for her. "It's complicated."

She waited, wondering if he was going to entrust her with further explanation or if the topic had been officially dropped. The blast of cool air-conditioning inside was jarring but welcome, and there wasn't as much of a crowd as she would have expected. The hostess promptly led them to a table. A two-sided chalkboard with the day's menu written on it served as the centerpiece.

"The problem with menus when you're hungry," Addie said, "is that it all looks good."

Giff nodded. "I can't—"

"*Giff!* Gifford Baker?" A woman's delighted voice cut across whatever he'd been about to say.

Addie turned to see a beautiful brunette approaching, eye-catching in an electric-blue dress and white sweater. The woman's hair was styled in a sleek bob. Addie caught herself just about to self-consciously smooth a hand over her own corkscrew locks.

Giff's mouth had fallen open in surprise. He didn't seem quite as ecstatic as the brunette, who'd reached their table by then. "Brooke. Hi. I wasn't expecting… How are… You look great, by the way. Marriage obviously agrees with you."

The woman blushed, turning away from him and toward Addie. "I'm sorry to interrupt so rudely. I'm Brooke McBride."

"Pleasure to meet you," Addie said, not at all sure that it was. "I'm Addie Caine."

Giff's eyes darted around the interior of the restaurant. "Is Jake with you?"

"Oh, no, he's pulling a twenty-four-hour shift at the station. I drove into the city to meet with a magazine editor. We just finished, actually, and I highly recommend the quiche."

By the time she'd stopped talking, Giff seemed to have regained his composure. "Well, it was certainly nice to see you. Tell Jake I said hi. I've been meaning to call him, but I've been busy with work." He made a vague hand gesture that included Addie. "New consulting job. Network securities. Addie and I were planning to talk shop over lunch."

"Oh, the two of you work together?" The corners of Brooke's mouth turned down, as though she were inexplicably disappointed by this news. "Then I'll let you get back to business. But, Giff, we will see you at the reception in a few weeks, won't we?"

"Of course," he replied jovially, his smile not fading until she'd rejoined her own lunch companion and they'd headed for the exit. In a strangely matter-of-fact tone, as if he were commenting on someone else's life, he explained, "That was my former fiancée."

And she's already married to someone else? Interesting. Addie had been given the impression that the engagement had ended fairly recently.

Seeing her confused expression, Giff flashed a self-deprecating grin. "Brooke eloped with Jake."

"Jake, your best friend Jake?" *Ouch.* Addie was at a complete loss for words. What Giff had been through made her ex look like a saint in comparison.

"What can I get y'all to drink?"

Having all but forgotten that they'd come here for lunch, Addie jumped at the waitress's question. "Um, just a glass of water for me, thanks."

Giff ordered a sweet tea. They lapsed into silence as they each studied the menu. Addie felt as if the unfinished subject of Giff's broken engagement was still hanging over them, but she couldn't think of anything to say that wasn't awkward as hell. Instead of quiz him on his own romantic woes, she decided to let him know he wasn't alone.

"I was engaged," she said. "At the beginning of the summer. Not so much anymore."

He seemed surprised by her out of the blue announcement, but then a lazy grin spread across his face. "Did he run off with your best friend?"

"No." She couldn't help chuckling at how appalled Jonna would be by that idea.

Giff winked at her. "Then I win."

They both laughed, dispelling the tension between them. By the time the waitress returned to find out what they wanted to eat, they'd decided to each order something different and share. Neither of them got the quiche.

"You asked earlier," Giff began, "if Jake and I are still close?"

Addie waved a hand to where Brooke had stood. "Guess that answers my question."

"Don't misunderstand, I'm not bitter toward either of them. It's just that our encounters have been a little... strained."

She was impressed by what had to be massive understatement. "You're being very mature about this. If my ex walked in here, I doubt I'd smile and tell him he looked great. Or maybe I would," she reconsidered. "But inside, I'd be thinking diabolically vindictive thoughts."

Giff studied her quietly. "You think you have the ability to be diabolical?"

She compiled a quick mental list of pranks that she and Zach had played on each other when they were young. "Absolutely." Raising an eyebrow, she cautioned playfully, "Don't underestimate me."

"Noted." The look he gave her was so speculative that she almost pointed out that she was only kidding, but he spoke before she had the chance. "So what did happen between you and your ex-fiancé? I realize it's none of my business, but since you know my story…"

"It was the kids," she said. "At least, that's the excuse he gave. As soon as he realized that I would become their permanent guardian, he became distant and it didn't take him long to call the whole thing off. Said that he wished me the best but that instant fatherhood wasn't in his plans."

Giff scowled. "Your fiancé left you on the heels of your brother dying? How long had you been with this jerk?"

The quick way Giff took her side was immensely cheering. "Three years. But he made the right decision. He really wasn't ready for parenthood."

"And you were?" Giff asked.

She knew it was meant to be sympathetic, not an indictment of her parental abilities, but she winced anyway because his question was the same one she'd asked herself every day since Tanner and Nicole had come to live with her. "I like to think I'm doing the best I can."

"Oh, I'm sure of it. I know I only saw you with your nephew for a few minutes, but… They're lucky to have you."

"That's what Jonna says—my friend Jonna Wilder. I think the two of you have met, actually." She continued when he nodded. "But I have trouble feeling like these two kids are 'lucky' in any way after what happened to them. Tanner's been swimming since he was three—used to be like a fish in the water—and since his parents drowned, water terrifies him. He can't stand mention of the beach, he's practically afraid to sit down in the bathtub!"

Aware that this was becoming too morbid a conversation for a quick workday lunch with the boss, Addie tried to smile. "You got any advice on overcoming fears? What kind of stuff scared you when you were a kid?"

"Making mistakes," he said. "That was far scarier than getting cornered by bullies."

"You had run-ins with bullies?" Looking at his well-built, six-foot frame, she couldn't imagine anyone picking on him.

"Once." He smiled at her. "Before my middle school growth spurt. But it ended in my and Jake's favor and never happened again."

She was more and more curious about this childhood friend who'd fought by his side, then later stole his girl. But after the unexpected encounter with Brooke, Giff probably preferred not to dwell on that situation any more today.

"So why the deep-rooted fear of making mistakes?" she asked instead. "Everyone does."

"Everyone should. I've managed to mostly avoid it, which means I never learned how to screw up gracefully, how to recover and move on." He stopped suddenly, grimaced. "Oh, Lord, did I basically just say that I never mess up? I sound like the most arrogant man in the entire state of Texas."

"Don't be silly. Texas is huge. Maybe the most arrogant man on the Gulf Coast," she said sweetly.

He snorted. "Thanks for the perspective."

Their food came, and they each set about divvying up portions for the other to try. Giff proclaimed it all good, but Addie barely tasted anything, her senses too concentrated on the man across the table.

"I think I worried about making mistakes because of my parents," he told her, signaling to the waitress for a drink refill.

"Were they the type who tried to help you succeed by pressuring you?" Addie knew plenty of misguided parents who might truly want the best for their children but drove them to anxiety attacks; Jonna's folks had been like that. Addie's parents had been more mellow, especially since she was the second child, but wanting to live up to her big brother's example had always been enough to spur her.

"No, my parents were wonderful. Damn near perfect," Giff said ruefully. "They loved each other, respected each other, adored me. I wanted to be just like them. My mother had breast cancer last year, and I was so... There were these moments where I didn't know what to say, how to make it better, but I was so sure that if Dad was still alive, he would've—"

Addie surprised herself by lifting her hand to the tabletop and lightly squeezing his fingers. "She's lucky to have you," she said, echoing his earlier sentiment. While she'd never met Mrs. Baker, it was obvious how much Giff cared for the woman and what mother wouldn't consider herself blessed to have raised a son like that? "I'm sure she appreciated everything you said and did whether it felt natural to you or not."

The words were soothing. Even though she sometimes

floundered with the kids, was the love behind her actions enough? Would they cling to that over the years and forget the accompanying awkwardness? She felt lighter, as if this conversation with Giff had eased some of the weight that had been pressing her down for the past month.

"There was one other thing," Giff began. "That I was afraid of? But I've never told anyone."

Her eyebrows rose. "Okay, now you have to tell me. It's not fair to dangle something like that and not follow through!"

"Promise not to laugh? Talking cars."

"Excuse me?"

"I was afraid of talking cars. My dad was an investor in this company, Lone Shore Innovations, and they held an annual convention. He took me when I was little, younger than Tanner. They demonstrated actual inventions and improvements for the home, but also ideas for the future. This was way before we all had e-mail and flat-range stoves. My dad was talking to some other men and I snuck off to check out this cool car. I was already feeling guilty for wandering off and I jumped about a foot when a low, computerized voice came out of the car. Probably just a recording on a motion sensor of some sort, but it sounded like an evil robot to me at the time."

Addie tried to smother a laugh, which only made it worse.

Giff shot her a wounded look. "It was very tragic. I had nightmares. Imagine my trauma when, a year later, *Knight Rider* debuted! But I was determined to face my fears."

She was laughing almost too hard to speak. "Dare I ask how?"

"After my parents fell asleep, I'd tiptoe into the garage and shut myself in there with the cars. At night. Just waiting for one of them to say something. I told myself I wouldn't be scared no matter what."

The image was both absurdly hilarious and surprisingly poignant, a barefoot little boy in pajamas, alone in the dark but resolute. "You should tell this story to all your potential consulting clients," she said. "It demonstrates your perseverance. Giff Baker, a man who gets things done."

The amusement in his eyes disappeared, his expression dimming as suddenly and completely as a lightbulb with a blown fuse.

"Did I say something wrong?" Granted, she'd been making fun of him and he'd warned her he was a proud man, but he'd also proven himself to be a man with a sense of humor. And she would have sworn he'd felt the same connection and camaraderie that she'd been enjoying.

"Not at all," he assured her, looking away. "You just reminded me that I have a job to do. We should get our check and go."

"Sure." He had a point. In fact, she should have been the one keeping an eye on the clock, so that she could go back in a timely manner. She didn't need to do anything else this week that might make her look like a slacker. "But thank you for lunch. I had a good time." The best time she'd had in...

Yikes, that long?

She couldn't even recall the last occasion she'd had to

sit and talk—maybe even flirt a little—with an attractive man. She assumed it must have been with Christian before their breakup, but their relationship had melded into a blur of familiarity. The single memory that stood out the most was of him holding her hand at Zachary's funeral, hardly a warm and fuzzy moment.

"Anyway, thank you. You're a good listener," she told him.

It boggled the mind—why on earth had Brooke walked away from a man who was smart, funny, good-looking, successful and compassionate? Giff was the perfect man! *For someone else,* she immediately cautioned herself.

For someone whose plate wasn't already full with work and family. Even worse than the potential disaster of dating a colleague would be for Tanner to get attached to another adult who eventually disappeared from his life. So where Addie was concerned, Giff was as out of reach as one of the millionaire mansions in the elite River Oaks neighborhood. Why tempt herself by standing at the edge of the property and ogling what she'd never have?

Chapter Seven

Seeing Brooke at lunch had deepened Giff's guilt that he'd been avoiding Jake, but shame wasn't the only reason he called the other man's cell phone as soon as he returned to the office. Every time he'd heard himself mention Jake to Addie, it had been a reminder of the long friendship they'd shared. The endless football practices that had paid off when their team won the state championship, the way they'd met and how Jake had always had his back. Knowing how hard Addie was trying to be there now for her niece and nephew made Giff think about his freshman year of college, when he'd found out his own father had died and how Jake, his roommate at the time, had tried so hard to be there for him.

Jake answered his phone, "McBride."

"Hey, you have any spare time tomorrow afternoon?" Giff said by way of greeting. "Been a long time since I kicked your ass in racquetball."

There was only the briefest of pauses before Jake snorted. His tone was every bit as flippant as Giff's had been. "Since *never*, you mean. Squeaking ahead at the last minute for a one point victory is hardly an ass kicking. But I could meet you any time after four if I need to refresh your memory."

A knot of tension that Giff hadn't even realized was in his chest eased slowly. He smiled into the phone. "I'll reserve the court and text you the time. I'd say bring your A-game, but we both know you don't have one."

"Who needs one when the opponent is you?" Jake returned cheerfully. "See you tomorrow, Baker."

GIFF WAS ALREADY ON THE COURT, practicing ceiling shots, when Jake arrived.

The dark-haired man looked paradoxically more tense and more relaxed than Giff was used to seeing him. The slight wariness in Jake's gaze and hesitation to his smile had never been there before when greeting his lifelong friend. But Jake's rigid, military bearing had eased and Giff didn't think it was only because time had passed since Jake's days in the Army. No, Giff would bet that the newfound calm in Jake's manner was due to marrying the woman he loved and the joy of having rediscovered his family now that his alcoholic father had finally quit drinking. Even as a wisecracking teen who'd been quick to help a buddy or charm a co-ed, there'd been an underlying anger to Jake. It was gone now.

"Good to see you," Giff said sincerely.

"Yeah?" Jake arched a brow. "I was relieved you called yesterday. It's the first time we've talked since I told you about the elopement. I thought maybe…"

Giff shook his head. "Brooke ended up with the right man for her. I couldn't be mad at you for that."

"Says the guy who decked me," Jake drawled.

"I meant, I couldn't *stay* mad at you," Giff corrected,

choosing to gloss over the night, weeks ago, when he'd lost his temper for perhaps the first time in his life. Definitely the last time. That aberrant loss of control had been disconcerting. "Didn't you guys get the card I sent?"

"We did, and your congratulations meant a lot to Brooke. She would be devastated if she thought she'd disrupted our friendship."

"Yeah, well, tell her no worries on that score." Giff swallowed, embarrassed by the unspoken sentiment of how important they were to each other. "Look, if you're done sharing your feelings, I came to play."

"Good by me. Best two out of three?" When Giff nodded, Jake asked, "Evens or odds?"

"Evens." They counted off and Giff displayed three fingers.

At the same time, Jake held up two. "My serve."

They were matched in skill level, neither having a clear advantage. Both of them hit the ball several times before the rally ended in a side-out.

"So Brooke said you were having lunch with a woman yesterday," Jake said, interrupting Giff's serve. Either his curiosity couldn't be contained or he was playing dirty, trying to distract his opponent. The former seemed more in keeping with his character. For all his trash talk, Jake had a strong sense of fairness.

"A coworker." *One I'm investigating.* He smashed the ball harder than necessary, with no finesse at all. What would it have been like to meet her under other circumstances? *Pointless.* They had very different personalities and lifestyles. "I'm doing a short-term job for Bill Daughtrie—you remember him from college? Addie works for him. End of story."

"You sure?"

There was something in Jake's tone that made Giff turn and look...and miss the ball, which bounced a second time. "Are you deliberately cheating?"

"Of course not! I wouldn't expect a little small talk to throw you off so badly. You play while chatting with clients all the time." Jake smirked. "Unless it's the girl we're discussing who's throwing you off. Brooke said it seemed like there might be a spark."

Giff rolled his eyes. "Then she either has an overactive imagination—not uncommon among writers, I hear—or she's suffering from a guilty conscience and wants to see me with someone." This time last year, Brooke had been a reporter for a small newspaper in Katy; being with Jake seemed to have inspired her creative side. Giff knew she'd been branching out into other writing endeavors.

"Okay, no more questions about the coworker." Jake bounced the ball a couple of times. "But you know you're welcome to bring a date to our reception." Since the two of them had eloped, they were planning a large party so that all their friends and family members could celebrate the marriage.

It was alarmingly easy for Giff to picture himself there with Addie on his arm, easy to imagine her in an evening dress instead of her office attire. He'd noticed, despite himself, that she had fantastic legs. And a smile that could light up a room. Of course, she'd have to find a sitter for the night and—

He frowned when he realized he was actually entertaining Jake's suggestion.

"I can't date someone from the office," Giff said, surprising himself with the statement. Jake had already agreed to drop the subject. So, was the additional protest for his friend's sake or for his own?

"You're a consultant, you work in a different office every month," Jake said. "If you won't date anyone you've ever worked with, doesn't that rule out like a thousand women?"

"Stop worrying about my love life and serve the damn ball," Giff said.

They began playing with renewed zeal. Giff pulled ahead by a couple of points, the second one courtesy of an impressive splat shot. But Jake was quick to catch up. At first, Giff was able to lose himself in the game, but his undisciplined thoughts returned to Addie and the temptation to tell Jake about her. After all, Giff and Jake had been discussing girls since they'd first strategized the best way to get dates for the sixth grade Valentine's Day dance.

In meetings, Giff encouraged people to think out loud; brainstorming often led to solutions that had subconsciously been there all along. Would it dispel the conflicting feelings he'd been having since asking her to lunch yesterday if he explained to Jake why Addie wasn't his type? Maybe, but he shied away from making the argument since Giff had been so sure Brooke *was*— and look how that had turned out.

Most of the women Giff had dated had reinforced his self-image. When Giff was with Addie, it was as if she created a distorted reflection. The stoicism that made him reliable and efficient seemed like a liability when he found himself unsure how to comfort a teary woman. His habitual drive for success, as he'd explained it to her, had sounded like colossal arrogance, closer to a flaw than an attribute. The fact that he'd once had childhood nightmares about a talking car had always made him feel stupid and he'd never shared that with anyone. But with Addie listening, it had been an endearing, if silly, anecdote.

"Dude, are you even playing?" Jake's exasperated tone was laced with amusement. "You do realize you've given away the last three points and that I'm about to win?"

"What?" Giff pinched the bridge of his nose with his free hand. "I guess I'm not one-hundred percent on top of my game."

"No kidding."

"This job Daughtrie hired me for is...slightly different than my usual. And, to tell you the truth, he can be obnoxious. I half wish I hadn't taken the contract."

"He can't be the only obnoxious businessman you've ever worked with," Jake reasoned. "But I've never heard you complain about a job before."

"Sorry to whine. Serve the ball."

"No, I didn't mean it like that. You never complain about anything. It's refreshing." Jake grinned. "Makes you one of us mere mortals."

Even though Giff knew his friend was exaggerating for comic effect, Jake's words struck a chord. Giff had been thinking that Addie made him see himself differently. But recalling his restlessness over the summer and recent unexpected moments like letting himself snap at an employer or asking Addie to lunch on a whim, he wondered if it was more than that. Was he changing into someone different?

The thought was strangely exhilarating.

Chapter Eight

Though her memory was blurred by a lack of sleep, Addie seemed to recall that there had been a time when she could arrive at a destination and simply get out of her car. Maybe she'd had to carry a laptop case or the occasionally heavy purse, but that was nothing compared to today's trek from the parking garage to the stadium. The diaper bag alone was stuffed with dozens of items—teething rings, toys, bottles of premade formula, infant-appropriate sunscreen, an emergency change of clothes, medicine to soothe the baby's sensitive stomach, gel to soothe the baby's sensitive gums, not to mention the wipes, disposable changing table covers, ointment for baby's sensitive tush, and the diapers for which the bag had been named in the first place. People climbed Mount Kilimanjaro with less gear than this.

Juggling Nicole's diaper bag with her own purse and pushing the collapsible stroller barely left Addie a free hand to hold on to Tanner and protect him from oncoming traffic. This was the first time she'd taken the kids into such a crowd by herself, and it was a bit overwhelming.

"Stay close to me," she reminded him. "Don't walk

away from me, even once we're inside the park. *Especially* once we're in the park."

"'Kay," he said, his voice subdued from beneath the brim of his father's old Astros cap. Already adjusted to its smallest setting, the adult-sized hat still fell practically past his eyes, but Tanner had begged to wear it. She'd figured it would help protect him from the sun. Out of deference to the heat, she'd worn a brick-red tank top with sand-colored shorts, but she'd started second-guessing her choice on the drive. She was unused to her IT colleagues seeing her so…exposed.

Oh, well. At least she looked loyal in the team colors. Though Addie and her brother had grown up outside of Houston, they'd been raised die-hard Astros fan. Their dad had driven them to the city once a season for a home game at the Astrodome. Nostalgically, she missed the old stadium but Minute Maid Park was impressive, combining modern technology with an old-fashioned feel. She looked forward to showing Tanner the train, which ran whenever the Astros scored a home run. She only hoped Tanner was awake to see it. After last night, it was possible he'd nod off to sleep as soon as they found their seats.

His 3 a.m. shriek, splitting the silence of her dark apartment, had given her chills. *Mama! The water's in my room!* Addie had bolted out of bed and rushed to him, expecting to find him thrashing around in his sheets. Instead, he'd been standing in the middle of the floor, eyes wide-open, flailing at a rising tide only he could see. The heartbreaking image had kept her from falling back asleep for hours afterward. It had been difficult enough to pull him free from the nightmare; it had been downright excruciating—when he finally realized where he was and began crying for his mother—to remind him that his parents were gone.

No sooner had they cleared the ticketing turnstiles and the security check (Addie resisted the urge to tell the guard searching the bags that Nicole's diapers were only dangerous *after* they'd been used) than Tanner declared himself to be "starving."

"You said we could get a snack," he said. He slid his cap back on his head and accompanied his reminder with the pitiful look of an underfed waif.

"I didn't mean in the first three minutes," she objected. She'd thought that in the event of a slow inning, she could help break up the time by taking him to one of the many concessions vendors. But if she started buying him drinks and food now, she'd be broke by the time the game ended. "You just finished lunch!"

En route to the game, she'd gone through the drive-through lane of a hamburger joint and let him eat in the car.

"I'm hungry again," he insisted, sounding so much like a stereotypically whiny small child that she almost grinned. She much preferred dealing with this than trying to explain to a confused child in the dead of the night why his mother and father weren't answering his cries.

"In a little while," she said firmly. "Not yet. Let's find our seats first, okay? And I should take your sister into the restroom."

The baby had obligingly slept for much of the ride, and now that she was awake, Addie had no doubt she needed to be changed. Unfortunately, the line at the "family" restroom was already pretty long.

"Why don't you just come with me into the ladies' room?" Addie said, turning toward the Women sign.

Tanner's bottom lip thrust out. "I'm too big to go in there. It's for girls."

The charm of his "normal child" crankiness was wearing off fast. "Tanner, there are way too many strangers here for me to let you out of my sight. This bag is heavy, and I'd appreciate it if you could get a move on."

Now that protruding lip was trembling and his brown eyes glistened with the warning of tears. "Daddy always took me in there." He was trying to pull her toward the men's room. "I'm a big boy now!"

Because this might actually be about missing his father and not just a tantrum over which bathroom to use, she kept her voice gentle. "You are a big boy, and I know your dad was proud of you. But he'd want you to listen and to be a big helper."

"Trouble?" asked a rich masculine voice from behind her.

Giff! She supposed that encountering him while she looked like a pack mule was no worse than how she'd first met him. "Hi," she said, looking over her shoulder. The bags and stroller prevented her from completely turning around. Though she wouldn't have believed it possible, Giff Baker looked even better in a T-shirt— *those arms!*—than in well-tailored dress shirts.

He smiled warmly at her. "Need a hand?"

"I can go with him!" Tanner announced. "He's not

a stranger. I met him. Remember me?" he demanded plaintively.

Giff looked perplexed but didn't lose his smile. "Sure I do, sport."

Addie sighed. "Tanner and I were having a difference of opinion over splitting up. I wanted him to come with me and Nic into the ladies' room, but he—"

"Ah," Giff broke in. "I understand. Want us to meet you right back here?"

She bit her lip, trying not to hear Jonna's voice in her head telling her how wonderful Giff Baker was. "You sure you don't mind?"

"It's no trouble at all," he promised.

"Thank you," she told him, choosing to ignore Tanner's soft but heartfelt "yay!"

She took the baby into the ladies' room, telling herself that she was not a bad parent who had given in to an ill-mannered child—*we reached a mutually acceptable compromise.* When she returned to the agreed upon spot, Giff and Tanner were already waiting.

"All right, now we're ready to find our seats," she told Tanner. She smiled at Giff. "Were you headed that way, too?"

He hesitated. "Actually, no. I got here early to watch batting practice, so I've been here awhile. I was searching out something to drink to cool myself down and maybe something to munch on when I ran into you."

Tanner looked up at his new friend, channeling a malnourished Oliver Twist, and moaned, "I'm so hungry."

Fascinated, Addie waited a beat to see if he was going to break into a chorus of "Food, Glorious, Food!" When he didn't, she reasserted her parental authority. "Snacks later, seats now."

Her nephew heaved a sigh. "Yes, ma'am."

She turned to Giff, unable to stifle an absurd temptation to defend herself. "I swear I've fed him today. Multiple times, in fact."

He laughed. "I believe you. Growing boys eat a ton. They're like locusts."

"My grocery bill weeps," she muttered.

Giff held out a hand. "Want me to carry that bag? I'll show you where we're sitting."

"You don't have to," she said, wanting to jump at the offer. Hadn't he just said he was going the opposite direction?

"I know that." He slid the strap of the diaper bag down over her arm, and she relinquished it gratefully.

Mr. Daughtrie had reserved seating in two consecutive rows of the mezzanine level. Giff stopped at the second row, where Pepper Harrington sat a couple of seats in.

Giff flashed her a megawatt smile. "Pepper, could you do me a big favor and scoot down? With this stroller, Addie should probably sit on the aisle. Everyone okay with that?"

There were good-natured murmurs from the few people who would be disrupted by the shift in seats. No one, including Pepper herself, seemed to mind terribly.

"My seat was in the front row," Giff said, "but I'll move back here."

She felt herself blushing. Though she welcomed Giff's presence—entirely too much—she didn't want him to think she was incapable of fending for herself. "It's all right. Don't feel like you have to babysit us."

"Not at all. I just like your company." He smiled down at Tanner. "We were right in the middle of a philosophical discussion about Darth Vader. Besides, I'm here by myself and I'm gonna need help eating my nachos later. Not to mention those giant pretzels—can't come to a game without getting a giant pretzel."

Tanner grabbed Addie's arm so tightly she worried about bruising. "Can he *please* sit with us, Aunt Addie?"

Her heart squeezed. On the one hand, she could well imagine how desperately her nephew yearned for time with a father figure. On the other hand...was it dangerous to let him get attached to Giff?

Lighten up, Caine. It's just a few hours at the ballpark.

"Of course we'd be delighted if you'd join us," she told Giff.

"Great, save my seat and I'll be right back."

"Deal." She arched her eyebrows, trying to look stern but pretty sure her grin ruined the effect. "But don't you dare come back with a giant pretzel for the kid."

"Wouldn't think of it," Giff said innocently.

The kid in question had already squeezed his way down the row, to where he'd spotted Gabrielle. Probably hitting her up for chocolate. But both Gabi and Tanner looked content with their conversation, so Addie took the opportunity to fold up the stroller and lay it down. She situated Nicole against her shoulder. Park policy was that one didn't need a ticket for infants, but they had to sit in a patron's lap.

"She's cute," Pepper said.

Addie whipped her head to the left, looking over Tanner's empty green seat to her nemesis. "Uh...thank you?" When was the last time Pepper had ever said anything nice to her without doing so to make herself look better?

But the wistfulness on Pepper's face looked sincere. "You may have noticed I'm career-oriented."

Addie snorted in agreement.

"And I like it that way, I don't want to lose my edge. But sometimes I wonder if it means I'm giving up my chance at *that*." She nodded toward the baby.

I'll be damned, Pepper Harrington's human after all. Addie smiled wryly at the other woman. "If there's one thing I know for certain about you, it's that you go after what you want. If you decide you want motherhood and your career success, you'll find a way to make it work."

Pepper inclined her head, looking grateful. "You're right, thank you. After all, if *you* can juggle them both..."

Well, Addie amended, *partly human anyway.*

A shrill giggle caught her attention and she automatically looked down at the row of Daughtrie employees in front of her. A long-limbed blonde with a girlish laugh and a high ponytail was seated next to Robert Jenner—although, considering how much of her body was pressed against his, they might as well be sharing a seat.

Addie's mouth dropped open. Confusion got the best of her, and she whispered, "That is definitely not the Mrs. Jenner I met at the Christmas party."

"You didn't hear that she left him?" Pepper asked matter-of-factly. "Can't say I blame her, given Robert's tendency to chase skirts. He's come on to every female in the company, including you."

That's news to me. Not entirely sure whether Pepper was serious—and not wanting to look foolish either way—Addie didn't respond. She did, however, mentally review several office encounters with Jenner. After her brother died, she remembered Robert had been extra kind to her—hanging out at her desk a lot, handing her a box of tissues on the particularly bad afternoon of Zach's birthday, declaring with enormous sympathy that she needed a hug and wrapping his arms around her.

Her jaw clenched. *That rat was using my grief to hit on me.*

Men!

Of course, not all guys were like that. Giff Baker, for example, was a credit to his entire gender. He returned midway through the first inning with a drink tray and an irrepressible smile.

"Take note," he told her. "Not a pretzel in sight."

"You got us drinks." Considering the heat of the day and the fact that she had a fifteen-pound warm-bodied weight snuggled against her chest, a cold beverage sounded like heaven.

"Sodas for us, a lemon slush for the little man." Giff nodded to the smallest cup. "That's legal, isn't it? I know you said no food yet and I wanted to respect your say-so."

"You are a *very* nice man," she said, beaming up at him. Their gazes locked and after a moment, the wholesome appreciation she was feeling toward him morphed into a more earthy admiration. He had gorgeous eyes and muscled arms that made a woman want to feel them wrapped around her. His profile in the sunlight was striking.

Giff finally tore his gaze away, muttering under his breath, "Not that nice."

Thankfully, the tension between them was broken when Tanner came running back to his seat, no doubt stepping on toes and jostling people as he went. "D'you think the Astros are going to win?" the little boy asked Giff. Any whininess he'd exhibited when they first got here had been completely replaced by wide-eyed enthusiasm. "I hope we score a lot! Aunt Addie likes to score."

Addie choked on her cola. "What?"

"When we played air hockey at Puck E. Pizza's, you did that dance every time you scored," Tanner reminded her. "It was funny. You should see it, Mr. Giff."

Giff's green eyes were lit with wicked amusement. "Believe me, I want to."

"You should do your dance when the Astros score a home run," Tanner decided.

"Absolutely," Giff agreed.

She glared at him before turning to her nephew. "It's kind of crowded here. But I tell you what—soccer starts this week. I'll do the dance whenever you make a goal. Okay?"

"Okay!" Tanner's face fell. "But then Mr. Giff won't get to see. Wait, d'you wanna come to one of my soccer games?"

Addie's heart raced. Hadn't she assured herself that

all this guy bonding was okay since it was only for the afternoon?

Rather than offer any glib promises, Giff appeared to be giving the matter real consideration. "I don't know. Thank you for the invitation, but your aunt and I will have to talk about it, make sure it's okay."

"Why wouldn't it be?" Tanner switched his attention to Addie. "It's okay with you, right? You like Mr. Giff!"

Addie had the sudden, evil wish that it would be a very, very long time before Nicole decided to start talking. Lord only knew what trouble the two of them could get her in. "Yes, of course I like him, but—"

"You don't mind if he comes?"

"Well, Tanner, honey, he's a very busy man and—"

"Too busy for me?" This time, the child looked genuinely upset and not guilty of overacting. It was inconceivable to him that his new best friend might not be equally eager to spend time together.

"No," Giff interrupted. "Not too busy for you, sport. When your aunt gets the game schedule, you guys pick the one you want me to attend, and I'll be there."

"Yay!"

Addie tried not to have the same reaction. It was dangerous to let herself be too happy over the thought of seeing Giff again. Trying to reassert some professional distance between them, she kept her comments to a minimum for the next couple of innings.

Apparently, Giff mistook her reserve for anger. At a moment when Tanner seemed distracted—he'd finally been allowed a snack and was plowing through an order of nachos—Giff leaned his head close to Addie's, speaking in a low voice. His breath tickled her ear.

"I'm sorry if I overstepped earlier," he murmured. "It probably wasn't my place to accept his invitation, but he gets to me, you know?"

She thought of her nephew's big brown eyes. "I know."

"So you'll forgive me?"

"I wasn't mad. I think it's very generous that you agreed to come to a game. You made his day. I just—" Her words were drowned out by the roar of cheering fans around them. Addie blinked. "I think we missed a home run."

"Woo-hoo!" Tanner was on his feet, waving his hands in the air. "Go Astros! Aunt Addie, you sure you can't do your dance?"

"Please," Giff added mischievously. "There could be a giant pretzel in it for you."

She pursed her lips. "I'm not that easy."

"I didn't think so." His mouth curved into a half smile. "But a man can dream."

GIFF'S ARM WAS TINGLING where he'd lost circulation, his T-shirt was plastered to his chest, his butt had gone numb in the stadium seat—and he was having one of the best afternoons of his life.

"You sure you don't want me to take her back?" Addie whispered. "I know how heavy she is."

Considering the cacophony of noise surrounding them, from the buzz of fans and crack of the bat to the periodic bursts of rock music intended to pump up the crowd, Giff found it adorable that Addie lowered her voice in an attempt not to wake the baby. It was probably a habit she didn't even know she'd developed, like the moments at the office where he'd noticed her swaying back and forth. While she'd been waiting for her turn at a vending machine on Friday, she'd been subtly rocking, the same way he imagined she often did with Nicole at home.

"She's fine," he said.

"You can't be comfortable."

Maybe not physically—the kid *was* heavy, and the day had just hit its high temperature. But he felt more at ease than he had in a long time.

When Nicole had started wailing earlier, Addie had gone through all the normal motions to soothe her. She'd fed her, gone to check her diaper and applied some kind of topical painkiller, explaining that the infant was teething. But nothing had worked. Addie had tried to suggest that maybe it was time for them to leave, at which point Tanner had burst into tears. Reluctant to see them go, Giff had surprised himself by asking if he could walk the baby for a few minutes.

"Just to give you a break," he'd offered. "If it doesn't help, well, then you can go."

Addie had tried to warn him off. "She's...volatile. I can't promise that she won't spit up on you. Or something."

He'd refused to wuss out in front of Addie over a little baby slime. "I'm washable."

Something intriguing had sparked in her eyes, and she'd looked away quickly. Maybe he was projecting his own suggestive thoughts on to her, but he'd suddenly imagined himself in a shower. With her. Belatedly, he tried to imagine a very cold shower.

It hadn't taken long for Nicole to drift off in his arms and he'd returned to their seats to find that Tanner, who'd been so vehemently opposed to missing the end of the game, had ironically fallen asleep, as well. The longer the boy dozed, the more he sprawled over his seat into his aunt's. Which meant that Addie had spent more and more of the game pressed against Giff.

The teams were currently tied, and Giff was hoping for extra innings.

From the other side of Addie came a snore that seemed far too loud for a first-grader, and she giggled. "Delicate, my nephew is not."

"He's not supposed to be," Giff said with approval. "Boys are rough and tumble and good at building tree houses and belching the alphabet."

She screwed up her face. "Ew. Poor guy. Not only can I not build a tree house, I can't even offer him any trees. We're stuck in my tiny apartment. He has no real space to run around. I've been trying to sell his parents' house, but you know what the market's like right now. And until we do, I'm pretty strapped. I— Sorry. I don't mean to dump this on you. I'm tired and babbling. None of us got any sleep last night."

Giff grinned over the top of her head at her snoozing nephew. "Did Nicole keep you all up?"

"Tanner, actually." Her voice was heavy with sadness. "He has nightmares, some nights worse than others. He kept dreaming that the apartment was filling with water."

There was a pain in Giff's chest. And he didn't think

it was caused by the way the baby was pressed against his rib cage.

"Woo-woo!" Seated in front of them, Robert Jenner whistled. From the man's slurred exuberance, Giff suspected the man had enjoyed a couple of beers with the game.

"What did we miss?" Addie asked, scanning the field.

But there was no action down there; play had halted for a coach's visit to the mound. The coach, pitcher and catcher were in conference. Glancing up at the video board that showed replays, special effects and crowd shots, Giff realized that Jenner's cheer had been a juvenile response to action on the KissCam, where the camera crews landed on random couples and the people in the stadium applauded—or ignored—their on-screen kiss. The televised image changed, and Giff stared, his brain slow to process that he was looking at *himself.* Well, him plus a snoozing Nicole and Addie, who was so close her head was nearly on his shoulder.

We look like a family. This was what he'd longed for, the fuzzy but tantalizing mental picture of a lovely, intelligent woman at his side and cherub-cheeked children. In his rush to realize this dream, he'd almost picked the wrong woman, but life—and Jake McBride—had given him a second chance.

Acting on impulse, he turned, lifting Addie's chin with his free hand. "We have to," he said with an unapologetic smile. "KissCam's an American tradition."

Her lips parted on a gasp, but she recovered enough to murmur, "I wouldn't want to be unpatriotic," against his mouth.

His lips claimed hers, causing a sweet, dizzying rush of heat and pleasure. *God, she tastes good.* He hadn't really intended to prolong the moment, but Addie's kiss had short-circuited his brain. He delved into her mouth, wanting more of her taste, more of *her,* and her fingers clutched at his arm. A husky moan sounded in her throat, so low that only he could hear. He was sure the camera had moved on by now, prayed that the camera had moved on, but he couldn't bring himself to stop. He wanted to lose himself in this kiss and never come up for air. He wanted—

"Mr. Giff, what are you doing to Aunt Addie?"

Chapter Nine

"Have you lost your damn mind?"

Very probably. Because instead of listening to Bill Daughtrie's Monday morning tirade, Giff kept peering toward the window, hoping to catch a glimpse through the partially opened blinds of Addie's arrival at work.

"HR is probably going to have a field day with your stunt yesterday," Bill continued from the other side of his desk. "Make us all take a seminar on sexual harassment or something. This isn't some spy movie! When I told you to keep a close eye on the two females in IT, I didn't mean sleep with them for information. Although I suppose I can understand why a pretty little thing like Ms. Caine—"

"Addie and I are *not* sleeping together," Giff bit out. "And finding your security leak was the furthest thing from my mind when I kissed her."

Bill raised his bushy eyebrows at that. "Maybe I had it wrong, then. People know you're here doing computer security work. If she's afraid you're on to her, maybe she's deliberately cozying up to you—"

"Oh, for the love of…Addie is not your traitor."

"Then you're finally starting to pin down electronic evidence?"

"Not exactly," Giff hedged. "But the main reason I ever considered her as a possibility was because she has those two kids to care for now. A grief clouded-mind and increased financial responsibilities might have led to desperate, out of character actions. But when I took a second look at that possibility, I realized the timeline made no sense. Her brother died fairly recently and you believe the first bids were sabotaged months ago."

"The 'reason' you considered her?" Bill echoed. "I'm paying you to consider everyone here, and you're letting personal feelings screw with your head. You need to stay away from Addie Caine."

Giff, used to being his own boss, narrowed his eyes at Bill. "Do you have a clearly delineated office policy forbidding employees to date?"

"No, but—"

"Then don't tell me who I can and can't see," he said with deceptive mildness.

"Well, hell, son."

And don't call me son. But Giff was too preoccupied by thoughts of Addie and what he'd say when he saw her to pick petty arguments.

After Tanner's interruption yesterday, Addie had sprung away from Giff as though he'd been on fire. *Which I definitely was.* Instead of answering the kid's question, she'd distracted him with a barrage of her own. "Oh, you're awake, honey? Do you want anything? More to drink? Do you need to go to the bathroom?" She'd then maneuvered it so that Tanner spent most of the rest of the game sitting between the two adults. But she'd stolen glances at Giff for the rest of the game and thanked him breathlessly "for everything" when they'd said goodbye.

Had she pulled away from him because she regretted their kiss or simply because of their young audience?

"Baker, you *are* paying attention, aren't you?"

"Of course," Giff said automatically.

"Good, because I think this is our chance. The contract for the Groverton job fell through—the engineering firm declared bankruptcy—and they've announced a short, emergency window for accepting bids to complete the project. I'll have my management team put one together this week. Since it's been such a challenge for you to find evidence months after the fact—" a hint of disdain crept into Bill's tone, suggesting that maybe the "challenge" was Giff's competency level "—maybe this will give you the opportunity to find the culprit before he, or *she,* erases her tracks."

Giff pondered this. "It could work, assuming the person pushes their luck by attempting it another time."

"Crooked people who've repeatedly gotten away with their crimes start to feel invincible," Bill said.

"I'll take your word for that, not being crooked myself."

Bill glared. "I think we're done for now."

"Yes, sir." Giff tried not to bound out of his chair with noticeable enthusiasm. He also restrained himself from making a beeline to Addie's desk. His sole compunction about that kiss they'd shared was that it had been in full view of her office mates. Would she be uncomfortable that they'd seen it? As a woman in a male-dominated field, she probably already felt as if she were under scrutiny. Giff's opinion was that they were consenting adults, temporarily working together at a place where there was not an antifraternization tenet, so there was no problem. However, he understood that she would remain here after he left and might feel differently.

Please don't let her feel differently.

As it happened, she wasn't at her desk. He found her in the break room, pouring coffee. He strolled in, keeping his voice and expression casual even though they were the only two people present.

"Morning, Addie."

She lurched at the sound of his voice, reminding him of the day they'd met, but her coffee didn't spill. And her tone was just as nonchalant as his. "Morning, Giff."

He crossed the small room, wanting to be close to her, wanting his arms around her without the sweet but awkward obstacle of Nicole between them. "I was hoping to talk to you…"

The fact that she quick-stepped back against the counter didn't bode well for them being on the same wavelength.

Giff stopped short, trying not to look as crestfallen as Tanner after being denied cotton candy. "I'm guessing you're not happy about yesterday."

"Are you kidding?" she asked brightly. "Yesterday was fantastic. Tanner and I had a great time—he fell asleep last night talking about it and then kept chatting on the subject all through breakfast. You were so great with Nicole and such a big help to me. And we won the game!"

"Addie," he said patiently.

She sighed. "Look, I've never made out with a co-worker before. And we're not even equals in the office hierarchy."

"You're sorry I kissed you."

For an unguarded moment, heat flared in her eyes and it was all the answer he needed. She'd wanted that kiss. At least part of her wanted to kiss him again.

Go for it, some unrecognizable inner voice prompted. Giff blinked. He certainly was not going to try to seduce an uncertain woman into changing her mind in the middle of their workplace! Since when did he even have thoughts like that?

"Addie, the last thing I want is for you to be uncomfortable around me."

"You don't need to apologize." A shy smile appeared like the sun from behind clouds. "I did kiss you back."

"Trust me, I haven't forgotten. I thought about it all night," he admitted baldly.

She blushed but didn't look away. "Me, too."

"Is it worth mentioning that we'll only be coworkers in the short run?"

"I'm Tanner and Nicole's guardian," she said gently. "And I'm in that for the long run."

"But I'm crazy about them. I'm not one of those guys who would run from the idea of dating a woman with kids."

"Tanner's already crazy about you, too. And… Look, he's been through a lot. Although he never really bonded with Christian, I had been with the guy since Tanner was a preschooler. He was used to him making an appearance at Christmas and such. They weren't friends, but

Christian was a constant. Tanner's lost all the constants in his life—his parents, his school, his home, his friends. I want you to come to his soccer game, I do, but how completely do I let him attach to you? If I dated you and things didn't work out, you'd be one more loss in his young life."

He could contend that maybe things *would* work out, but it seemed a rather psychotic argument to make, that she risk Tanner's emotional well-being on a "maybe" with a man she'd only known a week.

But perhaps after they'd known each other longer a lasting relationship would seem more plausible. Giff hadn't become successful in business by quitting at the first sign of adversity. All he needed were time and proximity on his side.

He gave her his most winning smile. "What are you doing this weekend?"

"Giff!"

"I'm not asking for my own selfish reasons." He placed a hand over his heart. "Well, not *just* for my own selfish reasons. How would you like some help making Tanner's nightmares go away?"

ACCORDING TO THE ROSTER on her clipboard, Addie was now the coach of eight first-graders—six boys and two girls—who comprised the Sea Turtles. So far, organizing their inaugural practice session felt like herding cats. Seven hyperactive cats and a sobbing kitten who wouldn't release his death grip on his mother's skirt. Buckled into her stroller on the sideline, Nicole watched the proceedings with avid interest, sort of an assistant coach who didn't speak much.

Addie wished other people on the field would follow her niece's silent example.

"But this is ridiculous," one father complained over the hubbub of assembled kids. "Did you look at the game schedule you just handed out? The Meteors, the Raptors…and we're the lousy Turtles? What kind of mascot is that? How are we supposed to beat a team like the Sharks?"

"Sir, you do realize that both teams will be made up of six-year-olds and not actual sharks or sea turtles?" She tempered her sarcasm with a chipper tone and dazzling smile; the combination confused him enough to temporarily shut him up.

"Now." She clapped her hands together and tried to project authority so that no one, including parents, challenged her, while also looking harmless and cheerful so that no small children would find her intimidating. Especially the kid who was now crying so hard he seemed on the verge of hurling. His mother was trying to pry his fingers away from her clothing and kept insisting from between clenched teeth, "This will be so *good* for you, Sammy!"

This particular league didn't use a goalie for games until the third grade bracket. Instead, Addie was simply supposed to put two kids up front on offense and two kids in back as defense, switching out players in regular intervals so that each child got approximately equal field time. *Whether he wants it or not?* She'd planned to let them get the feel for the different positions, then practice dribbling, passing and kicking but maybe that had been overly ambitious. Right now, she'd settle for getting all eight of them in one spot with no crying.

"Okay, everyone, huddle up!" The words felt unnatural and silly, but it had seemed like the kind of thing a coach would say.

And Tanner seemed to approve. Beaming, he was the first to join her in the center of the child-sized playing field. Everyone else followed suit except for the Team Crier and a boy and girl who were occupied in a shoving match about gender equality. Addie noticed that the boy's father was far more concerned about the team name than the fact that his obnoxious son had announced "girls can't play soccer." She supposed Mia Hamm was slightly before the little punk's time.

"Hey." She approached the two squabbling kids and pointed to the girl. "Your name's Bridget?"

The girl nodded.

"Nice to meet you. I'm Coach Addie, and all these kids are our teammates. Including this little boy…?"

"Caleb," he said defiantly.

"We support our team," Addie said sternly. "We work together and we don't fight amongst ourselves."

"But he said girls can't play soccer," Bridget balked.

Addie bent her knees, squatting to the boy's eye level. "*I'm* a girl. Do you think you can beat me at a one-on-one soccer game, Caleb?"

He glared but moments later shook his head in defeat.

Thank goodness. There was a slim chance he could have beat her, and then she really would have been up a creek. "All right, then I guess we're all agreed that girls can play, too. Now, everyone. Huddle. Up." She asked for a quick show of hands to see who had ever played soccer before, then said they were going to learn some basic terms and do a few drills.

The other little girl—not Bridget—shot her hand into the air. "Is this an 'assessment'? Last spring we did skills assessment. You don't have to asses me. I'm good at all of it."

"Well, humor me anyway—" Addie checked her list "—Mandy."

For the entire second half of practice, Addie kept one eye on her watch to see if it was time to quit. Jonna would meet her here after work; they planned to grab dinner somewhere near the fields. By the time Jonna arrived, Addie's main restaurant criteria had become "Is it still happy hour anywhere?"

Jonna grinned as she helped Addie load practice balls and orange cones into the trunk of the car. "Rough first day, Coach?"

"Aunt Addie was terrific!" Tanner said. "We're gonna win every game."

Addie considered her lineup and winced. "Honey, you know the point is to have fun, get exercise and develop good sportsmanship, right?"

Tanner nodded. "And *win*."

Jonna chortled.

"Are you gonna come watch me play?" Tanner asked her.

"Absolutely. Is it okay with you if I bring my boyfriend? He likes sports."

"Ab-so-lutely," Tanner echoed back at her. "Aunt Addie's gonna bring *her* boyfriend, too."

Jonna stopped dead in her tracks.

Addie smiled weakly. "I can explain."

"Okay, enough stalling," Jonna chided. "You've made me wait long enough."

The closest restaurant to the soccer fields had been a little hamburger place that served great malted milkshakes but no cocktails. They'd eaten there, with Addie hissing that the Giff conversation was best saved for later, and then Jonna had followed them back to Addie's apartment. Now that the kids were in bed and Addie had opened a bottle of wine, there was no more avoiding the topic.

"So you're Giff Baker's girlfriend?" Jonna squealed, nearly sloshing white wine onto Addie's couch in her glee.

"No, of course not." She deliberately made it sound as if the idea was laughable, but it wasn't. Not after this morning, with Giff telling her that he'd been thinking of her kiss and reminding her that they wouldn't be working together for more than a month or so. Girlfriend seemed a rather adolescent term, but he'd definitely been interested in pursuing some sort of relationship. *"I'm not one of those guys who would run from the idea of dating a woman with kids."*

"Giff and I have become friends this week," she began, sipping her riesling to buy time.

"Close friends?" Jonna drawled.

Close enough that I could tell you how his lips feel. Firm and coaxing, but not pressuring or invasive. He didn't push, he simply made a woman want to surrender herself into his embrace.

"Daughtrie had the annual Astros day that he always does for office morale or employee bonding or whatever. Tanner and Nicole and I ended up sitting next to Giff.

You can imagine how much Tanner ate up the chance to hang out with a guy. The two of them really took to each other. And…I'm afraid Tanner might have gotten the wrong idea about Giff and I because of the KissCam."

"The what?"

"You know what I'm talking about. You've been to hundreds of baseball games. That thing where they zoom in on some couple and—"

"You and Giff?"

"Jonna, you're going to wake up the kids if you don't take it down a notch."

"Sorry. Didn't mean to shriek." Her friend looked abashed for a millisecond before her voice rose again. "But are you telling me that you kissed Giff Baker?"

"Yeah, but it was no big deal." *Liar!* "We were just following the custom, like kissing someone under mistletoe or the Italian double-cheek kiss."

Jonna's eyebrows rose. "And did he kiss you on the cheek?"

No, he frenched me and I was so caught up in it that I momentarily forgot about thirty thousand fans, including my nephew and my boss. Addie's face tingled with heat and she knew a blush stained her fair skin. That was more than enough answer for Jonna.

"Adeline Marie Caine! And you didn't call me last night to share any details? Never mind, you probably spent the evening reliving nirvana." Jonna fanned herself with her hand. "So that explains why Tanner might think Giff's your boyfriend. Where did he get the idea that Giff was coming to watch him play soccer?"

"Tanner asked him to, Giff said yes."

Jonna looked suitably impressed. "Nice guy."

"Really nice guy." Addie hadn't even worked her way around to telling her about Giff's brainstorm today, on how he might be able to help Tanner overcome his water phobia. But even though it looked as if she would be spending Saturday with Giff, that was to help her nephew. It wasn't a romantic date.

She cleared her throat. "Giff and I talked today at work and he understands that dating can't really be my priority right now. Not with the kids."

Jonna frowned. "Your brother adored you and he would have wanted you to be happy, like he and Diane were. I get the whole setting a good example thing, I do. You should probably refrain from public pole dancing—"

Addie snorted.

"But I don't think Zach would have wanted you to live a lonely, nunlike existence. There are other single moms out there in the world and some of them date."

"I'm not saying I'll never go out with a guy for the rest of my life," Addie clarified. "But, Jonna, it's only been a month. Tanner's still pretty fragile and it would be easy for him to glom on to Giff. Plus I already feel torn in too many directions, trying to fit soccer games and PTA meetings and pediatrician appointments into my work schedule. I don't have the time or mental energy that developing a relationship takes, that a guy like Giff deserves."

Jonna bit her lip. "I disagree."

"There's a shock," Addie said affectionately.

"Don't think of a man as one more responsibility, think of him as someone to help ease the burden of all your new responsibilities." She grinned. "It's amazing what a really good orgasm can do to relieve stress."

"I am not having sex down the hall from those kids with a man I've only known for a week!" No matter how tempting it sounded. "No more wine for you. It gives you kooky ideas."

"You're cutting me off after half a glass?" Jonna pouted. "First no details about the kiss, now no booze. What else do you plan to withhold?"

She'll find out sooner or later. "Well, I *was* keeping to myself the news that Giff and I are taking the kids fishing this weekend."

Jonna's face went slack with surprise. "You and Giff, together? The guy you're not dating?"

"He has a former client who owns a luxury motor boat. Giff's a big believer in facing down your fears, and he thinks this could be fun and therapeutic for Tanner. I wouldn't have attempted it by myself, especially since I don't have access to a boat, but hopefully Giff's presence will calm Tanner down. He'll be excited about doing something with his new buddy and being around a big strong guy may bring out his macho instincts. He might want to show Giff how brave he can be, which should help us get him on the boat. It's a highly generous favor Giff's doing for us, but it's not a date. It's more like that Big Brothers program. This is for Tanner, although I haven't told him about it yet."

"You're going to spend a sunny Saturday at sea with one of Houston's most eligible bachelors and you honestly believe it's just for Tanner?"

When you put it that way. "Um...more wine?"

AT WORK, GIFF AND ADDIE had strategized the best way for Tanner to hear about the boating trip. Addie believed that if they told him too soon, it would give the boy too much time to build up the fear in his mind. He would have had nightmares all week. She and Giff had come up with a solid plan, one that had her eyeing the phone while she and Tanner ate hot dogs for dinner Friday evening.

As ever, Giff did not disappoint. The phone rang at five-twenty and it occurred to her that, when it came to depending on someone, the man she'd known less than two full weeks was proving to be more trustworthy than the one she'd been with for three years.

"Hello?"

"Addie." He made her name an endearment. "It's me."

She smiled broadly, not bothering to censor her expression the way she did at work, so it wouldn't seem too familiar, too happy. "I know."

"I'm looking forward to seeing you tomorrow. Have I mentioned that imagining you in a bathing suit tomorrow has been one of the highlights of my week?"

She laughed. "I doubt the reality will match the fantasy. It's a pretty pedestrian one piece."

"Not in my head it isn't. You'd look great in a string bikini."

The hell she would—but it was sweet that he thought so. Rather than admit she was flattered by his view of her, or, worse, succumb to the temptation to stay on the phone flirting, she took the sensible path. "I should get Tanner for you."

"All right," he said affably. "I'm looking forward to seeing him and Nicole again, too."

He really sounded as though he meant it, and she was touched. She'd felt over her head at first, especially when Christian left, thinking that she was all the kids had. That initial panic was finally starting to fade. She may be their guardian, the main person in their lives now, but their environment was expanding to include other stable role models, too, adults who cared about them. Giff and Jonna, teachers and caregivers, Heidi Lee the elementary school counselor, Gabi Lopez who had suggested Addie bring the kids over for a play date sometime. Addie inhaled deeply, feeling truly peaceful for the first time in a long time. *They're going to be okay.*

"Tanner, honey, Giff is on the phone and wants to talk to you."

The way the little boy's face lit up simultaneously warmed her and justified her concerns that Tanner might get too attached to her project leader. Tanner leaped out of his chair, his stocking feet making him skid across the kitchen tile.

"Slow down," she cautioned, carrying the cordless phone to the couch. She sat next to Tanner so that she could remind him to actually speak into the receiver—during calls with her parents, she'd noticed that he sometimes held the phone out in front of him, as if it was one of his toy walkie-talkies. He snuggled against her, and she was close enough to hear Giff clearly when he said hello.

"Hey, sport. You have a good week at school? No more trouble?"

"No, sir." Tanner shook his head very solemnly. "I got all happy faces on my chart."

"Good job."

"Are you calling about watching me play soccer?" Tanner asked.

"Not exactly, but I'll talk to your aunt about that later. You know how you invited me to a game? That was really nice, and I thought I'd return the favor, invite you to do something with me. Would you like to do something together tomorrow?"

"Yes!" Tanner whooped. He slanted a look at Addie. "Can Aunt Addie come, too?"

"Her and Nicole, the whole family."

Even though she knew what he'd meant, making her reaction completely irrational, Giff's words rocked Addie. *The whole family.* It was all too easy to picture the four of them together. Giff, with a smiling Tanner on his shoulders, Addie next to them, carrying a happily gurgling Nicole.

"I have a friend," Giff was saying, "who owns a really nice boat and he offered to take us all out fishing. Have you ever been fishing before?"

"Once. My dad took me." Tanner cuddled more deeply into Addie's side, his expression conflicted.

"Did you have fun?" Giff prompted gently.

"Yeah."

"Would you like to try it again?"

The boy's soft brown eyes were wide. "Dunno."

"Tanner, I really think we'd all have a good time if you come with me. We had a great day at the baseball game, didn't we?"

Addie could feel her nephew's body relax slightly at

the happy memory and mentally congratulated Giff on redirecting the topic to something less threatening. Giff Baker may be known for his understanding of technology, but he was also damn good with people.

The boy's voice was barely a whisper when he admitted, "I'm scared."

Addie tightened her arm around him, hugging him close.

"That's okay, sport. Everyone gets scared."

"Even you?"

"Even me. But your aunt will be right there to watch over you, and I'll be with you, and Captain Jason has life jackets for all of us, even Nicole. I won't let anything happen to you."

Tanner swallowed, looking nervous but determined. "Okay. I'll see you tomorrow."

"Thanks. I'm proud of you, sport."

Addie pressed the heels of her palms against her eyes so that she wouldn't have to explain to her nephew why she was crying.

"You want to talk to Aunt Addie now? I'm gonna go finish my french fries." Barely waiting for a response, Tanner thrust the phone out to her and happily scampered back to the table.

She sniffed. "You were great." If Giff asked her to go out with him right now, she'd say yes. Right at this moment, she'd agree to pretty much anything he asked.

"*He* was great," Giff said modestly. "That's a good kid you're raising."

Her chest tightened. "I know. But it's hard sometimes and they don't come with programming code and I can't thank you enough for the way you helped with this. I owe you."

"Enough to consider a string bikini?"

She gave a watery chuckle. "Good night, Giff."

"That wasn't technically a no," he pointed out as she disconnected the call.

After she'd hung up, she remained still for a long moment, unable to ignore the growing truth. *Who am I kidding?* She'd told Giff and Jonna that there was a real danger of Tanner becoming too emotionally invested in the man. It was a real risk, trusting your affection, your heart, to someone else. Yet it wasn't her nephew sitting here now, counting the hours until they saw Giff in the morning.

She was the one on the verge of falling.

FREE Merchandise is 'in the Cards' for you!

Dear Reader,

We're giving away FREE MERCHANDISE!

Seriously, we'd like to reward you for reading this novel by giving you **FREE MERCHANDISE** worth over **$20**. And no purchase is necessary!

You see the Jack of Hearts sticker above? Paste that sticker in the box on the Free Merchandise Voucher inside. Return the Voucher promptly...and we'll send you valuable Free Merchandise!

Thanks again for reading one of our novels—and enjoy your Free Merchandise with our compliments!

Pam Powers

Pam Powers

P.S. Look inside to see what Free Merchandise is **"in the cards"** for you!

-AR-09/10)

We'd like to send you two free books to introduce you to the Harlequin® American Romance series. These books are worth over $10, but they are yours to keep absolutely FREE! We'll even send you 2 wonderful surprise gifts. You can't lose!

REMEMBER: Your Free Merchandise, consisting of **2 Free Books** and **2 Free Gifts**, is worth over $20.00! No purchase is necessary, so please send for your Free Merchandise today.

Plus TWO FREE GIFTS!

We'll also send you two wonderful FREE GIFTS (worth about $10), in addition to your 2 Free Harlequin® American Romance books!

Order online at:
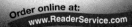
www.ReaderService.com

Chapter Ten

Addie scowled at her reflection. *Vanity, thy name is woman.* Despite the times she'd maintained that she and Giff should be no more than friends, with ten minutes to go until he was due to pick them up, she found herself wishing she was, well, sexier. The man spent time at high-dollar benefits and symphony orchestra performances with beautiful socialites in designer evening gowns. Compared to those women, she probably wasn't very alluring in her pink-and-white checkered halter bathing suit and denim cutoffs.

She half wished she owned a string bikini. Granted, she wasn't endowed enough to fill out the top portion very well, and she'd never had washboard abs, not even at eighteen, but her arms were toned, her legs were great and— *Knock it off! You're not* supposed *to be alluring.* Not for this outing, anyway.

Resolving to put aside her ego, she grabbed a wide barrette and secured her hair in a ponytail as she walked down the hall. "Tanner? Giff will be here soon, and it's been a few hours since breakfast." How was it that the child she had to drag out of bed on school mornings cheerfully got up with the sun on the couple days she could have slept in? "You want a snack, honey?"

"No, thanks." He glanced up from the cartoon he was watching. "My tummy doesn't feel so good."

Nerves, no doubt. Yet he'd never once asked or suggested that they cancel the day's plans. She was so proud of him she ached with it. Joining him on the sofa, she ruffled his hair. *You look so much like your daddy.* She had a moment of déjà vu—how many Saturdays as a kid had she sat with her big brother on the couch watching cartoons, laughing, bickering? "Did I ever tell you about the time your dad talked me into painting myself blue?"

Tanner's eyes widened. "Really?"

"I used to watch this cartoon about a village of little blue creatures who lived in the woods, and your father told me that they were real but you could only see them if you were blue like them."

"And you believed him?" Tanner asked incredulously.

"Give me a break, I was little! And he wasn't much older than you. Grandma was not happy with us."

Tanner giggled. "You're making this up."

"If I were going to make up stories, I wouldn't be the one doing foolish things in them. Trust me." She hugged him, glad she'd shared the silly, miscellaneous memory. Although she would never discourage the kids from talking about their parents, she rarely brought up Zach and Diane because she hadn't wanted to upset Tanner. But maybe that had been a mistake.

"Hey, you know who else you can trust?" she asked after a moment. "Giff. He's a good guy. If he says we're going to have fun today, I believe him. What about you?"

Tanner considered this, then nodded.

"Good. Now if you'll excuse me, I have to finish packing our duffel bags." As she stood, she glanced to where Nicole was gurgling and kicking her feet inside a mesh-walled playpen. "Tanner, promise me you'll never try to get your sister to paint herself blue."

"I promise." His voice followed her into the kitchen. "What about purple?"

Chuckling, she rummaged through the two open bags on the table, trying to inventory what she'd already packed and what she still needed. She was grabbing some extra granola bars and bottles of water when there was a knock at the door.

"I'll get it!" Tanner volunteered.

"What do you always do first?" she prompted.

"Look through the peephole," he said with a long-suffering sigh.

Ever since the kids had moved in, she kept a small plastic stool to the side of the door so that Tanner could check before he unlocked or opened the front door. Though Giff was expected, she figured the safety precaution was an important habit to develop.

"It's him!" Tanner called.

Addie heard the metallic click of the dead bolt, followed by Giff's deep voice. The sound caused the same bone-deep yearning she experienced whenever she passed the Dessert Gallery over on Kirby Drive. *Yummy.*

"Hey, sport. I like the swim trunks." The two guys

Texas Baby

discussed their favorite superheroes for a moment, then Giff asked, "Where's your aunt?"

"In the kitchen. She's filling our dusting bags."

Footsteps approached and Addie glanced up, meeting Giff's smile with her own. "Duffel," she said.

"I figured." He leaned against the end of the counter, watching her.

Her apartment wasn't spacious by any stretch of the imagination, and having the former football player stand in the entrance to the room shrunk the kitchen considerably. Not that she felt crowded, just that the room suddenly seemed more…intimate than it should.

She tried to lighten the mood—or, more accurately, her reaction to him—with a wisecrack. "I was going to wear one of my many string bikinis, per your request, but turns out they're all in the dirty laundry."

Giff studied her, doing a slow head-to-foot that raised her body temperature at least ten degrees. "I'm not disappointed."

Recalling her earlier wistfulness over not being "sexier," she suddenly found herself very relieved that she wasn't. If he was already looking at her with that much sensual appreciation…

"You're very good for a woman's ego," she said, her voice husky in her ears.

"I'm good for a lot of things." He grinned. "For instance—anything I can do to help you get ready?"

"Not really." It would be quicker for her to gather the one or two remaining items she needed than try to explain to him where they were. She laughed. "Unless you want to change Nicole's diaper for me before we go."

"Sure," he said amiably.

"Seriously?" Damn, he really was the perfect man.

"Why not? I mean, in the interest of full disclosure, I've never changed one before, but I should be able to figure it out."

"It's a good thing you're starting with a baby girl. They're the basic model. Boys are the advanced class."

Giff laughed. "Got it."

"She has a portable changing table out in the living room. Tanner can show you where it is and talk you through the process. I'll be out in a sec."

"Okay. Tanner," he said, as he returned to the living room, "can I get you to be my wingman? I've been sent on a diapering mission."

ADDIE'S LIVING ROOM WAS a clear statement on the two halves of her life, Giff noticed. Since he was no longer in her line of vision, he took the opportunity to be nosy and look around, wanting to learn more about the woman who was coming to mean so much to him.

The neatly arranged built-in bookshelf contained software manuals that were alphabetized and collector's editions of sci-fi DVDs; apparently her career interest in computers and technology spilled over into the books and movies she liked. She'd made the most of her limited wall space with two framed pieces of coordinating modern art by a painter whose work he recognized and enjoyed. But the order evident in the top half of the room was missing below. Random toys were present on the sofa, the corner of the entertainment system and the floor. There was a broken crayon under the coffee table. From the grooves in the carpet, it was obvious that she'd rearranged her furniture, scrunching it together to accommodate a baby swing, diapering table and playpen.

This single room of her apartment illustrated just how dramatically her situation must have changed, the havoc that could be caused when a single woman had to squeeze two kids into her life and home where one could argue that there wasn't really space for them. Yet he'd never once heard her complain or sound put out by the adjustments she'd made; the only frustration he'd heard her express was worry for the kids' well-being. Right below a framed, gallery-worthy painting hung a thumb-tacked drawing of stick figures playing soccer. He smoothed a finger over the sheet of paper. This room might be cluttered, but it was also a lot cozier than his professionally decorated home.

"That's a picture I drew," Tanner said. "It's not where the diapers go."

Giff glanced down, confused. "What?"

"You said you were s'posed to be diapering," Tanner reminded him.

"Right you are." Guessing that the first thing he needed for changing a baby's diaper was the baby, he went to the pen and lifted Nicole into his arms. She looked up at him with gray eyes that were almost exactly like her aunt's, except Nicole's gaze was filled with unconditional trust. There was none of the wariness he saw in Addie's gaze as she continued to second-guess how close she should allow Giff.

Giff smiled at the baby's uncomplicated joy to see him. "Could you put in a good word for me?"

Babies were, from a physical engineering standpoint,

odd. For something that looked so small, Nicole was solid through and through. He'd almost forgotten since the baseball game how much she weighed. Yet despite her heft, she didn't hang like a sack of a potatoes in his grip. She was mobile and practically boneless as she waved her arms in unnatural directions and tilted her head so far back to grin at her brother that a future as a contortionist seemed assured.

When Giff reached the table and started to lower the baby, Tanner interrupted.

"You're supposed to put down a pad first." Tanner pointed to the shelf of supplies beneath the tabletop.

"Oh. Thanks. I've never done this before." Holding a squirming Nicole against his shoulder with one hand, he used his other to grab a disposable changing pad. Unfolding it single-handedly took a moment.

"We're always putting stuff down for her to lay on and sit on," Tanner said. "Even at the grocery store. She has a special thing she sits in so she doesn't get germs from the cart. And Aunt Addie's always wiping things off before Nicole touches them."

Giff nodded absently. Now that he had Nicole lying on the appropriate pad, he was trying to unfasten the snaps at the bottom of her pink cotton outfit. Which would be a lot easier if her legs weren't flailing about as though she were auditioning for a revival of *Riverdance*.

"It's weird all the stuff grown-ups do to keep babies from getting dirty," Tanner observed, "when babies are usually the ones making the mess. You should have seen what came out of her diaper yesterday!" The boy shuddered.

"Uh…" Slightly unnerved by Tanner's words, Giff

wondered what kind of mess he was about to find. If it was bad, surely there would have been some kind of olfactory warning?

Having finally unsnapped what she was wearing, he was ready to tackle the actual diaper. He exchanged glances with Tanner, who was giving them the same skeptical, assessing look Giff had received at sixteen from the DMV employee who'd tested him for his driver's license. One of the adhesive tabs took its job too seriously and would not open, so he simply ripped the side of the diaper.

"Now you roll it into a ball and put it in there." Tanner gestured toward a disposal canister that looked complicated in its own right.

"Okay." Giff was listening to Tanner's instructions for twisting the top of the trashcan device when he realized that Nicole had flipped onto her tummy and had raised herself up onto her hands and knees. She immediately began rocking back and forth so forcefully that, for a horrified second, he was afraid she could launch herself off the table. He gently rolled her onto her back and grabbed a new diaper. She tried twice more to return to her stomach. It should have been a simple thing to hold her still except that it took more than the two hands he had to keep her in place, use the wipe, secure the new diaper and refasten her outfit.

"Boy." Tanner grinned. "You're really not good at this."

Giff winced. A former college honors graduate and high school valedictorian, and now he was receiving legitimate criticism from a six-year-old. Having small children around was a humbling experience. Addie must have a lot of inner strength to deal with it.

Of course, Addie was probably a hell of a lot better at this than he was.

ADDIE TOOK HER TIME IN the kitchen just so she could continue shamelessly eavesdropping on the two guys in the other room. But it sounded as if they were finished now. She zipped up the duffel bags and grabbed the sunglasses that were sitting atop yesterday's mail on the counter.

When she rounded the corner to the living room, she was treated to the sight of Giff cradling Nicole against his chest. It was a simple, domestic moment, but there was something so elementally beautiful in a virile man smiling at the pink-clad bundle he held that Addie lost her breath. Giff was imprinting himself on her heart as indelibly as the kids had.

Over the top of Nicole's head, Giff grinned at her. "Mission accomplished. All ready?"

No. She was not ready, not prepared for these burgeoning feelings. But she was becoming less and less confident that she could continue fighting the inevitable.

Chapter Eleven

Addie glanced down the pier at the stately white boat that was docked. The shiver of apprehension that went up her spine was unexpected.

"You okay?" Giff asked softly.

"Y-yeah." It hadn't occurred to her that Tanner might not be the only one nervous about his first time back on a boat. She hadn't spent nearly as much time aboard them as her brother had; in fact, he was in almost every shipboard memory she had.

"This is hard for you," he said.

She looked back at Tanner, not wanting him to hear that his aunt was scared. "Lots of memories," she said finally, swallowing hard. "I was so focused on what this would be like for him, I didn't... Back on the horse, though, right?"

"Or in this case, sea horse." Giff accompanied his pun with a crooked smile that sliced through her melancholy.

"Thank you." If she weren't encumbered by Nicole's bulky carrier, she might have thrown her arms around him in a grateful hug. Instead, she turned her attention back to the waiting boat, frowning at the words on its side.

"Shiver Me Rum?" she asked blankly. Interesting choice for a vessel name. "What exactly does that even mean?"

"Did I warn you that Captain Jason is a little eccentric?"

"Fair enough. I wasn't entirely sure what a *timber* was, anyway."

A dark-haired man in khaki shorts and an unbuttoned Hawaiian print shirt waved at them. "Baker! Good to see you. And your friends." He reached down to give Addie a hand, relieving her of the bags and cooler she carried before helping her up on the boat. "It's especially nice to meet you, Ms…?"

"I'm Addie Caine," she said. "Thank you so much for doing us this favor."

"Jason Marcos. And no thanks necessary. Always happy to help a beautiful woman." He gave her a rakish grin. "Giff did tell you I was richer than him, right? Better-looking, too, but you can see that for yourself."

The blue-eyed man with his teasing smile and tanned face was definitely attractive, but Addie didn't respond with the flare of interest she might once have. *Giff's ruining me for other men.*

Giff snorted. "Too much time in the sun, Marcos. You've baked your brains."

Jason winked before helping Tanner board. "You must be Tanner. Giff's told me all about you. Want to be my first officer for the day?"

Tanner squinted. "Is it hard?"

"Nah. You can help me steer and be in charge of deciding when it's time for lunch."

"Okay."

Giff handed Nicole's carrier over to Addie, then hopped aboard the boat.

"All right," Jason said. "First order of business, life vests!" He lifted the cushioned tops of a couple of bench seats against the railing.

It was a nice boat, and a beautiful day to be on the water. The sky overhead was a bright, endless stretch of blue, punctuated by the occasional cottony cloud. Sunshine was reflecting off the rippling surface of the water, but the breeze kept it from being too hot.

"Want some help?" Jason offered Tanner. "I've got two that might be right for you. Let's check them out and see which one fits best."

Meanwhile, Giff selected one for Addie, holding it open for her the way he would a lady's coat at the end of a dinner date. She slid her arms through the holes, backing toward him, noticing that she could still detect the scent of his skin and soap beneath the tang of the water and the pervasive smell of liberally applied sunscreen. It was an act of supreme discipline to stop before their bodies met, to keep from leaning her head back against his chest. In reality, she subtly stiffened, holding herself but an inch away. In her mind, she tilted her head back to look into his eyes, to study that mouth that had enchanted her so thoroughly last Sunday, to give him access to kiss the smooth, sensitive line of her neck. She trembled with want.

Rescue came in the form of Jason. "Addie, you need

any help getting one of these on Nicole? I have a couple of choices for her, too."

"Yes, thank you." She quickly walked toward the other man, glad to have something to occupy her before she did anything stupid. Like throw Giff down on the deck and try to seduce him.

Once they were all appropriately buckled into the life jackets, their captain announced that the next item on the prevoyage agenda was, "Tunes. Reggae, Buffett, or the soundtrack from *Pirates of the Caribbean?*"

Addie laughed at the selection. "Buffett works for me."

They seated Tanner between Giff and Addie—she couldn't help noticing the way Tanner held on to the man's hand—and Jason started up the boat. They headed for deeper waters to the rollicking tune of "Cheeseburger in Paradise."

"I know a great cove for fishing," Jason informed them loudly, over the combined noise of the wind, music and engine. "It's not too far, and it's not usually crowded. I'll turn off the CD player and switch to the trolley motor before we get there, so we don't scare all the fish away. We'll be there in a few minutes."

"You hear that?" Addie asked her nephew. "We'll be there really soon."

Face pale, he nodded.

"Are you looking forward to fishing?" she asked, trying to distract him from his fear.

"I guess." The words were barely audible.

"You and I are going to catch *lots* of fish," Giff boasted. "Way more than your aunt Addie."

She arched an eyebrow, but it was difficult to look

stern instead of smiling at the way Tanner's expression had slowly eased. "Big words, Baker. Tanner, tell this goofball that your aunt is going to fish circles around him."

Giff smiled down at the boy. "Well, no matter who catches the most, the end result will be the same. Fish dinner tonight, mark my words."

ADDIE FINISHED ATTACHING her lure, then grinned up at Giff. "You know that fish dinner you're planning?"

"Did I say dinner?" His eyes danced with amusement. "I meant fish appetizers."

She cast her line one last time. "Dude. We couldn't even put together an amuse-bouche." Jason was the only one who'd so far put a fish in the cooler they were taking back, although Giff had struggled to reel in something that had ultimately snapped his line.

"Doubting Thomasina," Giff quipped. "Day's not over yet. We still have, what, another fifteen minutes?" Jason had told them he'd need to return them to shore no later than three-thirty because he was emceeing a children's cancer benefit tonight.

"Silly of me," Addie said, "to discount the massive quantities of fish we're going to catch in the next quarter hour."

"At least your nephew's rocking and rolling." Giff shot Tanner a fond glance. The little boy stood a few feet away, fishing rod in hand. He didn't use the boat's built-in rod holders that the adults utilized between casts.

Although the little boy had ultimately decided that he wasn't quite ready to go into the water yet, he'd relaxed a lot in the last couple of hours and was having a wonderful time. Addie knew that the afternoon had been therapeutic for him and suspected that coaxing him into the pool at her apartment complex would be much easier after today.

"What's he caught now, six?" Giff asked.

Her lips twitched. "Something like that."

Everything Tanner had excitedly reeled in had been too small to keep; Giff and Jason had explained that the fish had to be thrown back. A couple of times, Tanner's line had got another bite so soon after he'd released his catch that Addie wondered if it was just the same fish. Maybe one who was depressed and determined to end it all or, on the other end of the spectrum, a fish of undying optimism, convinced that *this* time the bait wriggling on the hook wouldn't be a cruel lie. Fortunately, Tanner hadn't seemed to mind that he hadn't actually kept anything.

"I did promise the kid seafood," Giff said. "Since we're striking out here, let me take you two out to dinner. I know a great place not far from your apartment."

She was glad she'd tossed changes of clothing into one of the bags. "Sounds wonderful." Truthfully, it sounded preferable to cooking their own fish. She didn't mind the activity of fishing—even on slow days, there was a certain cathartic, meditative quality in the casting and reeling—but cleaning the fish once they were caught? Ugh.

Dinner out with Giff sounded like the perfect capper to the day, as long as she could stay awake. Right now, one glass of wine would be enough to put her out. She was almost boneless, mellowed from the warmth, the gentle rocking motion of the boat and the sweet, sweet sound of her nephew laughing. If Tanner were being quieter, there was a slight chance they could have caught more, but she didn't care. She wouldn't trade his joyous outbursts for anything in the world.

Neither she nor Giff had reeled in anything worth keeping by the time Jason announced that it was time to stow away the gear and return to the dock.

"Tanner, you want to come help me turn the boat on," the generous-hearted man offered. "I'll show you how everything works."

"Awesome." The boy scurried after him.

Addie's throat was tight with emotion.

"Are you all right?" Giff stood at her side, peering at her with concern.

The words didn't seem adequate enough, so she threw her arms around him instead, hugging him. With barely any hesitation, he wrapped his arms around her, pulling her closer.

"Thank you," she whispered up at him. "For today. For everything." Even for the way he made her feel.

While she still questioned on some levels whether it was wise to fan the flames of the attraction between them, she felt alive and hopeful and connected, no longer adrift. She couldn't regret that. It was a tragedy that her brother had died so young, and it would be a disservice to his memory if she let fear keep her withdrawn, too cautious to seek happiness or let herself experience life fully.

Stretching her calves as she went up on tiptoe, she angled her face and captured Giff's lips in a kiss that was every bit as hot and tangy and playful as their day on the water had been. He raised a hand to tunnel in her hair, deepening their kiss, then pulling away just enough to suck at her bottom lip. Need hummed within her, thick and urgent. Their tongues met and tangled, and Addie couldn't help imagining how good his kisses would feel all over her body.

From what seemed like miles away, Tanner grumbled, "Aw *man,* they're doing it again. Kissing is so gross!"

Jason guffawed. "Give it a few years, kid, and you might feel differently. Kissing's not so bad."

Not bad? From Addie's perspective, it was pure, soul-deep bliss.

WHEN THE WAITRESS BROUGHT Tanner his plate of popcorn shrimp, she asked if he needed any cocktail sauce to go with it.

He wrinkled his nose. "No. Just ketchup. Thank you," he added at Addie's pointed glance. She watched him dig in, recalling the way he'd barely picked at his food when he first moved in and smiling at his rediscovered appetite.

"When I was a little boy, I loved ketchup," Giff told them. He was seated across the round table from Addie. They'd placed Tanner and Nicole, in a high chair, seated between them.

With Giff right across from her, Addie had a natural excuse for watching him through dinner without feeling self-conscious. The day she'd first seen Giff, she'd thought immediately that he was one of the handsomest men she'd ever met. Even with that high standard as a starting point, he still seemed to become better-looking the more she got to know him.

"My mom could tell you stories," Giff continued,

"about the Year of Ketchup. I was four and I wanted ketchup on *everything*. Not just the normal stuff like hamburgers but eggs, macaroni and cheese, ice cream—"

"Ew." Tanner laughed. "Ketchup on ice cream? That's even grosser than kissing."

His reference to the kiss earlier caused Addie to blush in memory. Peering from beneath her lashes, she found Giff studying her, desire clear in his eyes, and her blush intensified.

"Your mom is still alive?" Tanner asked.

"Yeah. She was really sick for a while, but she's better now. My dad's dead. He went to heaven, just like yours," Giff told him, his gaze meeting the boy's in a moment of man-to-man kinship Addie couldn't duplicate.

"Do you miss him?" Tanner asked, his voice trembling.

"Every day. But I try to do things that I know would make him proud and that makes me feel closer to him."

Tanner thought this over, then nodded soberly.

"I think it would have made your father proud that you were brave enough to get on that boat today," Giff told him.

The little boy sat taller, expanding under his hero's praise.

"My mom's been away on a boat," Giff said in a more casual tone. "One that's lots bigger than Captain Jason's. The ship she was on can carry more than a thousand passengers."

"Really?" Tanner sounded as dumbfounded as if Giff had said a million.

"Really. If you ever meet her, maybe she can tell you about her cruise." He turned to include Addie in their conversation. "You ever been on one?"

She shook her head. "I've only lived vicariously through Jonna. She went on one a couple of years ago and came back regaling me with stories about the midnight buffet." And her hot flirtation with the parasailing instructor, but that conversation wasn't fit for a minor's ears. "To tell you the truth, I'm not really a seasoned traveler. I've only been outside the state of Texas a few times. You?"

"In the last couple of years, I've been on the road a lot," Giff said. "My friend Jake gives me a hard time. He loves to see new places and whenever I get back he'll ask about local points of interest or great restaurants in the area, but half the time the only places I saw were the inside of my hotel room, the client's office and whatever bar and grill happened to be midway between. I guess it never occurred to me to seize the opportunity to sightsee because…I never had anyone to share it with."

That seemed lonely to Addie, but she didn't want to say anything that sounded like pity.

"So if you could go anywhere in the world," he asked her, "where would it be?"

She nibbled her bottom lip. "I can't pick just one. I would love to go to Italy…see Rome, eat lots of pasta. But the Louvre's in Paris. And I've never been to the Grand Canyon."

"I know where I'd go," Tanner volunteered. "Mars! I want to see if any aliens live there."

The conversation turned to NASA and the city's

Space Center. Tanner had never been and Giff matter-of-factly offered to take him someday.

Catching himself, Giff stammered, "If that's all right with your aunt, that is."

"*Please?*" Tanner pleaded. "It sounds awesome."

Addie nodded. "We'll find a day when we can all go." As she said it, she discovered it was no longer difficult to picture Giff as part of their future.

In fact, it was becoming much harder to imagine a future without him.

ADDIE UNLOCKED THE FRONT DOOR while Giff, carrying Nicole, and a sleepy Tanner stood behind her. Once she had it open, she instructed Tanner, "Go brush your teeth, honey. I'll be there in a second to get your pajamas."

"Okay," he mumbled agreeably. He started to pass her, then stopped, studying the two adults. "My mom and dad used to kiss a lot."

"Yeah?" Addie asked cautiously, not really sure where he was going with this but hoping it didn't result in something uncomfortable like asking Giff to be his new daddy.

Tanner nodded, looking unbelievably nostalgic for someone who'd only been alive six years. "I was thinkin'… Maybe kissing's not so yucky."

Touched to have his blessing, Addie leaned toward him. "Well, in that case…" She kissed him on the forehead with an exaggerated smack of the lips.

He giggled.

"Night, sport." Giff squeezed the boy's shoulder and they both watched him scuffle tiredly down the hall.

"That is one kid who is going to be asleep in seconds,"

Addie predicted. "Now, wish me luck with the other one."

Nicole had been good-natured through dinner, not too fussy, but definitely wide-awake after an extended nap on the boat, alert and chattering her favorite nonsense syllables. Addie took the baby from Giff.

"Tanner and I will be drawing thank you cards for Captain Jason tomorrow," she told him. "It was an amazing day. I wish…"

"Yes?" Giff prodded, seemingly prepared to make her every wish come true.

She averted her eyes. "I wish I could invite you in."

He tipped her chin up. "Something changed today. You changed your mind…about us?"

"Yes." She still had the kids to think of—she didn't want to rush into anything she'd regret later—but there was no more pretending that she didn't want to explore a relationship with this man.

He flashed a heart-stopping smile before leaning in to kiss her good-night. "You won't be sorry."

GIFF COULDN'T REMEMBER the last time he'd overslept— back in college, he supposed. But last night, after he'd dropped Addie and the kids off at her apartment, he hadn't been able to stop thinking about her kiss, the way she'd shocked him on the boat, how right she felt in his embrace. The unmistakable desire in her expression when she'd admitted she wanted to invite him inside. In an attempt to distract himself before the images made him crazy, he'd fired up his laptop and worked until just before dawn.

And now he was late. He'd promised to help

Jake today with a do-it-yourself home improvement project.

Without bothering to shave, he threw on a pair of jeans and an old T-shirt, then grabbed a cup of coffee for the road. As he drove, he realized that the last time he'd been to Jake's place had been the night he'd gone out there to give his friend his blessing to woo Brooke. When she'd broken up with Giff, she'd worried that dating Jake would cause too much strife between the two men. But Giff had realized, belatedly, that she was not the right woman for him and hadn't wanted to stand in their way.

Had he now found the right woman? Heading to Jake's house now felt as though he'd come full circle.

He'd no sooner climbed out of his car than Jake appeared on the front porch.

"Hey," Jake called. "I was debating calling your cell."

"Sorry," Giff said sheepishly.

Jake shrugged. "Sunday's your day off, don't want you to feel like you have to punch a time clock. It's just that, with you being Mr. Punctual, I wondered if I should worry."

"Overslept," Giff said. "I was up pretty late."

"Let me guess, working late?"

"Guilty." But not because he was a stuffy businessman with no other interests in his life—quite the opposite.

"Well, come on in," Jake invited. "You just missed Brooke."

"She didn't leave because I...?"

"Not at all. She and some friends are throwing a surprise baby shower for Kresley today, and Brooke's

the decoy, the one who made plans with her and is supposed to lure her to the party site later."

Mention of the shower made him think of Nicole. It
had been a challenge to change her diaper while she'd
been kicking her legs and gurgling, but he'd managed.
Even though she couldn't communicate yet like her endearing older brother, the baby girl had captured his
heart. Her cinnamon-colored tufts of hair and blue-gray
eyes matched Addie's coloring almost perfectly. If Addie
had a baby of her own, would it look like Nicole? He
knew she sometimes felt anxious about raising the kids,
but she would be a terrific mother. *She already is.*

"You okay there, hoss?"

Giff caught himself. He was standing on the front
steps of Jake's porch with a goofy grin on his face,
thinking about Nicole's baby powder smell and that
grin that made her look as if she knew a great joke she
couldn't wait to share with the rest of the world.

"I'm great. Although maybe I could use some more
caffeine before you let me near power tools," Giff said.
"So just how complicated is screening in a porch?"

"Piece of cake," Jake said.

"Which might be reassuring if I'd ever actually made
a cake."

"Never too late to learn. When your mom gets back,
you should ask her to teach you." Jake smiled fondly.
His adolescence—and Giff's—had been full of Grace
Baker's homemade brownies, cheesecakes and cobblers.
"When it comes to baking, Grace is about the best damn
chef in the country."

"In the world."

"She e-mailed, by the way," Jake said. "Told me she

gets home this week and will be at the reception Saturday. She sounds like she's doing great."

"No one deserves to be happy more than her," Giff said softly. His mother was a kind, intelligent woman who'd weathered the loss of her husband and, later, cancer with rare class and good humor. Come to think of it, Addie had a lot in common with her. When he'd first met Addie, all he'd seen was the superficial hysteria, catching her on a bad day and making snap judgments about her overemotional state. But now that he knew her better, he'd seen her strength and compassion. He admired her.

Jake poured them each a cup of coffee and they talked about the fire station, Jake's parents and the upcoming college football season. It was on the tip of Giff's tongue to mention Addie, but, after insisting during the racquetball game that there was nothing between them, he wasn't sure how to introduce the topic without a humiliating "Turns out, you were right, I was wrong." No guy wanted to say that. Even when it was true.

They headed to the garage and Jake explained that they were in luck because his patio was a concrete slab. "If I had a wooden deck, we'd have to worry about insulating a floor, but we're already a step ahead. Two, actually, because of the roof overhang for a shaded porch. All we have to do is the support beams and screening. Well, and wiring, but I'm saving that for another time with some of my EMT buddies. Brooke insisted they be on hand in case I electrocute myself."

Giff chuckled. "She's a very bright woman."

The two men were in the process of measuring screen panels when Giff's cell beeped in his pocket.

Reflexively, he dropped his end of the tape measure and grabbed the phone. "Oh." Just a text from Daughtrie, asking if there'd been any unauthorized network activity since the Groverton bid had been finalized.

Jake smirked. "You expecting an important call? Last time I saw someone move that fast, it was a buddy in the service and he was being shot at."

"I'm not expecting anyone. But," he added, "it would be nice to hear from Addie. You remember the coworker you asked me about?"

"I remember I tried to ask you about her, and you shut me down."

"Well, the situation's evolved." Yeah, that sounded good. Nothing he'd told Jake a week and a half ago was untrue. The facts had just...changed in the interim.

Jake picked up a couple of wood screws. "So you've rethought your position on dating coworkers?"

"I changed my mind about it faster than she did. She wasn't sure she was looking for romance. She has her hands full with two kids."

Jake whistled. "That's a fair amount of baggage."

"Everyone alive has baggage. Besides, you don't equate two great kids with cumbersome suitcases. Nicole's an adorable baby girl, not quite to the crawling stage yet. Tanner is a precocious six-year-old who's not afraid to tell me when I'm inept. And he's a big Astros fan."

"I like him already," Jake said with a laugh. "How's he feel about Aggie football?"

"Those children she's raising are really special. *She's* really special." Giff looked at the person who was as close as a brother would have been and admitted, "I might be falling in love with her."

"What?" Jake froze. "Giff. Come on."

"Thought you'd be psyched. You were the one pushing the idea last time we saw each other."

"Yeah, but—" Jake set down the tools he'd been holding and pressed his hands against his temples. "You said it yourself, a week and a half ago, you thought dating her would be a bad idea and now you think you're in love? It's déjà vu all over again."

Giff stiffened. "What the hell is that supposed to mean?"

"There's a disturbing pattern of behavior here. Look, I know how much you want a family. You hated being an only child, you still miss your dad and you personally have a lot to offer a wife and kids. Enter this woman with a ready-made family…"

"You make it sound like I care about her because she's *convenient*," Giff accused. "Is that really how you see me?"

Jake raised his palms in front of his chest. "I don't want to fight with you, especially not surrounded by saws and power drills. But you don't think this is a little bit like before, asking Brooke to marry you when you'd only been dating a few months? Now, after only a few weeks, you think you're fall—"

"This is nothing like Brooke," Giff swore. "She was the total opposite. We'd been together for a few months and on paper we made so much sense as a couple that it only seemed logical to take it to the next step. I never felt conflicted. I never felt in over my head or passionate about her.

"No offense," he added, recalling that this was Jake's wife he was talking about. He hadn't been implying any lack on Brooke's part.

"None taken." Jake met his gaze squarely. "Matter of fact, if you said you felt passion for my wife, we might have to have words."

"How long did it take you?" Giff challenged. "When did you first know you were falling for Brooke? And even after that, didn't you originally reject the idea of being with her?"

"You know I did," Jake retorted.

"So you admit that just because a man tries to deny the attraction or fight his feelings, that doesn't mean they aren't there."

Jake shook his head. "I think it's great if you have feelings for Abby—"

"Addie."

"And she returns them." He stopped. "Does she return them? You said she wasn't looking for romance."

"It found her anyway." Giff recalled the sweet stab of relief that had pierced him last night when she'd said she'd changed her mind about them. "I promised her she won't be sorry."

"That's a hell of a guarantee to give this early," Jake warned. "You ever think about starting slow, maybe just asking a girl to the movies?"

Giff glared. His friend's attitude was unbelievable. *You'd think since he broke up someone else's engagement, he'd be the last person to dole out unsolicited dating advice.* "Back off, McBride."

They returned to their support beams and worked in

silence for a while, but Jake was too blunt a person—and they'd been friends too long—for him to remain quiet.

"Maybe she is the perfect fit for you," he conceded. "I hope so. I want you to find what I... I want you to be happy. I overreacted. When you first started talking, it sounded like you were trying to recapture the dream, hop right back on the road to your white picket fence family goal."

"That's not it," Giff insisted.

But his mind picked that traitorous moment to recall what it had been like to see himself on the stadium's giant digital screen with Addie and Nicole. He'd had the sensation that he was staring at a snapshot of what he most wanted. They'd looked like a family, and he couldn't deny the thrill that had given him. Could there be a grain of truth to Jake's qualms?

Was Giff falling simply for the woman, or for all that she represented?

Chapter Twelve

When Addie got to her desk Monday morning, she was more than a little surprised to find Pepper Harrington waiting for her. *This can't be good.*

She nodded to the other woman. "Pepper. How was your weekend?"

"Not as divine as yours, I'm sure." The brunette's smile was caustic. "I overheard you and Giff last week, discussing your sailing plans."

Last week, she might have tried to explain the whole platonic backstory of her nephew's phobia, but she doubted it would ring true, considering she had kissed Giff. Again. Instead, she said simply, without animosity, "That's none of your business. If you have reason to believe my work is slipping somehow or that Giff is showing some sort of favoritism toward me, then you're within your rights—in fact, you're practically obligated—to report me to HR. Or to Bill. But until then…"

"Wow." Pepper looked almost proud. "I've never mastered that."

"Mastered what?" Addie said, forced to finally walk around the other woman just to get to her own chair.

"Telling someone to get lost without sounding bitchy," Pepper said. "You'll have to teach me sometime."

"Uh, sure."

"Here's the thing, Caine. People are talking about you and Giff. The two of you might have thought you were subtle last week, with your chance encounters in the break room, leaving within ten minutes of each other for lunch—"

"We're not having a torrid affair," Addie interrupted wryly. "We've had lunch together twice. But even if it were more than that, the man kissed me in front of an entire baseball stadium. It's not exactly sneaking around."

Pepper waved a perfectly manicured hand. "What's actually going on between the two of you isn't really the point. It's more about perception, and it's ticking me off. Do you know how hard I work in this office? And I don't want to be your BFF, but you pull your weight, too."

"Gee. Thanks."

"We're always busting our butts to prove ourselves among them, and *why?*"

"Them who?"

"The men in this office! Bill Daughtrie, who's so condescending half the time that I expect him to pinch my butt and call me darlin'. And Jenner, who has become such a sad, sad midlife cliché."

"The teeny-bopper he was with at the game?"

"That and his shiny new sports car. Have you seen it?" Pepper rolled her eyes. "Textbook. At least when a woman has a breakdown, she finds ways to make it interesting. And then there's Parnelli." She started in on another member of the IT team.

"Wait, I like Parnelli. He's sweet."

"He rents a garage apartment from his mother. Loser," Pepper declared, proving her own point about always sounding bitchy. "Anyway. I'll admit, I was annoyed about you and Giff at first, but then I vented about it to my friends."

Pepper has friends?

"The consensus was, you're not actually sleeping with him to get ahead."

Addie was appalled. "Of course not!"

"Because," Pepper continued, not appearing to have heard her, "if that was your plan, you'd be after Bill, not our consultant. So you guys, be happy. I think you should date if you want to, to hell with what the boys think."

Addie might have made some flippant comment, like "now that we have your go-ahead, I can live with myself again!" but she realized the woman had gone out of her way to be kind. The Pepper version of kindness, anyway. "Thank you."

Pepper nodded. "I got your back."

DURING THE MONDAY MORNING team meeting, Addie was proud of the balance she struck. She was never going to do anything as unprofessional as throw her arms around Giff in the office, but her unexpected talk with Pepper had led her to the resolution that she would stop sneaking around, from an emotional standpoint. When Giff walked into the room, instead of looking away and hoping no one saw what she was feeling in her gaze, she hit him with the full force of her smile.

He blinked, seeming dazed for a moment, then grinned back at her with such warmth that her pulse fluttered madly beneath her blouse. After the meeting, she took her time leaving the room, so that she was left alone with Giff. It wasn't subtle, she knew, but she'd decided Pepper was right. Let other employees talk— who cared? Addie had always been a diligent worker bee, untouched by minor workplace controversies such as who had overindulged at the Christmas party open bar or who was looting office supplies from the closet for personal use. But she'd never been as happy in her pristine past as she was now.

"Hi," she said. "I was wondering if you'd like to have lunch with me today?"

"You have no idea how much," he said, regret tingeing his voice. "But I've been summoned to have lunch with the big man. And I'm taking off tomorrow afternoon to pick up my mom at the airport, so I'd planned to work through lunch. How's Wednesday work for you?"

"I'll put it on my calendar." She thought of Pepper's comments earlier, about people noticing when they were both out of the office at the same time. "I have to leave early tomorrow, too. Soccer practice. Tanner is so excited about you coming to his game Thursday night."

"Wouldn't miss it for the world," Giff said. He grinned. "I've always had a soft spot for watching lady coaches in action."

"Really?"

"When I was in seventh grade, I had a huge crush on Coach Gwendolyn Dodge. She was in her twenties and worked with the junior high school volleyball teams and girls' track team," he reminisced fondly. "In fact, she may have been my inspiration for joining organized sports in the first place. Ever since Coach Dodge, there's something about a woman with a clipboard and a whistle that gets to me."

Addie didn't actually have a whistle. She made a mental note to get one before Thursday's game.

GIFF BLINKED AT THE WOMAN approaching the baggage carousel where he waited. If she hadn't waved and called out to him, how long would it have taken him to recognize his own mother? He supposed in his mind he'd expected a woman in a sensible pantsuit that wouldn't wrinkle on the plane. Instead, his mom was wearing a brightly colored tunic that was a riot of reds and yellows over a pair of capris. She'd replaced, temporarily at least, her usual pearls with a long strand of turquoise stones and her designer purse with a straw handbag.

"You look different," he told her as he closed the distance between them.

She poked him in the arm. "That had better be a compliment."

He grinned at her imperious tone. "Oh, it was. You look good." Healthy, happy. She'd gained a couple of much needed pounds. Once she'd finished all her chemo treatments nearly a year ago, she'd stopped looking skeletal, but her appearance had continued to be far too frail for his peace of mind. "It's damn good to see you, Mom."

"Language," Grace Baker chided with a raised eyebrow.

He laughed. "Yes, ma'am."

"Oh, I missed you!" Grace, who barely stood as high as Giff's shoulder, swept him into a tight hug. Her light, familiar perfume wafted over him, carrying years of memories in its scent. "Have you grown? Maybe I'm having a senior moment, but I swear you look taller than when I left."

Her comment triggered a random recollection of the narrow paper chart they'd taped on the back of his bedroom door, measuring his life in feet and inches. He recalled his triumphant shout when he'd reached the height requirement to ride AstroWorld's XLR-8 coaster. Did Tanner have a similar growth chart somewhere in Addie's apartment?

Giff grinned at her. "I'm pretty sure my growth spurt days are all behind me." Although, he had to admit, ever since Addie had smiled at him like that at the office yesterday—as if she were crazy about him and wanted the world to know it—he did feel as if he were walking a bit taller.

Suitcases and trunks were beginning to thud onto the silver conveyor belt. Giff and his mother moved closer so they could watch for her bags.

"So how are you doing?" he asked her.

Though her hair had turned an elegant silvery-white in the past decade, her blue eyes had remained exactly the same since his childhood. Now they twinkled knowingly. "Is that a 'how are you,' tell me all about your wonderful trip, or 'how are you,' are you still free of cancer cells and when's the last time you talked to your oncologist?"

"The first, of course." But he'd be lying if he said he

didn't sometimes think about the other and send up an extra prayer for her continued good health. It had looked bad there for a while. He'd feared he was going to lose the one person who'd been a constant his entire life.

"You worry too much about me, Gifford. I'm healthy as a horse now. It's time for you to turn your attention elsewhere. Find a nice girl and start a guilt-free life of your own without worrying that there's no one to take care of me."

He grunted a noncommittal response. The last two times he'd wondered if he'd found that girl, his so-called friend McBride told him he was making a mistake. "Let's collect your luggage, then I'll buy you a late lunch. Anywhere you want."

"A place with a nice light salad," she said, looking momentarily sheepish. "You would not believe how much they feed you on those cruise ships."

An hour later, they were seated at a table for two in a quiet restaurant that featured a gourmet salad bar. His mother had loaded up a plate with raw fruits and vegetables, and Giff had thrown together a taco salad.

"I bought you souvenirs," his mother told him.

"Judging from the number of suitcases we dragged to the car, I'd say you bought all of the Bahamas and Key West," he teased.

"I needed a wide variety of things," she said primly. "I was gone a long time."

"I know. I've been by the house regularly to water the plants, check messages, make sure your mail and newspaper delivery was stopped as requested."

"And I appreciate it, dear, but that's the most boring

update I've ever heard," she complained. "I want to hear the fun stuff!"

He laughed at her tone—it wasn't much different from Tanner's pleading when he wanted something that the adults around him were being too dim-witted to provide. "Fun stuff?"

"I've been gone for weeks, son. Please tell me you did *something* fun while I was gone."

"Let's see." He pretended to think it over. "I played some golf, went to a baseball game, took on a new client, changed my first-ever diaper—which wasn't fun, per se, but you would have found it entertaining—and I went fishing. Oh, and met a girl."

Grace's eyes glowed with pleasure. "You met a girl? And you just now got around to telling me? Brat."

"Should I have met you at the airport with a printed sign? Something that read Welcome Home, Started Seeing Someone While You Were Gone."

"Is it serious enough that she warrants a sign?"

He chuckled. "Serious enough to warrant a giant hi-def video screen."

But his mother wasn't listening. She was apparently replaying the rest of what he'd said. "You changed a diaper? Did someone we know have a baby? Or is this new girl of yours a single mother?"

"Single aunt. Addie has custody of her niece and nephew because their parents died."

"Oh, how terrible for them."

"They've been through a lot," Giff agreed, "but Tanner's a resilient little guy and he's already doing better in school and at making friends than he was a couple of weeks ago. He's six. The baby, Nicole, is five months old."

"This Addie must have her hands full," Grace said. "Will I get to meet her this weekend at Jake and Brooke's reception?"

"No." Giff chose his words carefully. "Even though Jake encouraged me to bring a date, I think the situation could prove…awkward."

Especially if Jake let Addie know about any of his misgivings. She'd already overcome her own doubts, and Giff didn't want her to have any reason to question her choice. In a flash of insight, Giff realized that although he'd found it relatively easy to forgive Jake for his part in breaking up his relationship with Brooke, Giff wouldn't be nearly as tolerant if Jake caused a rift between him and Addie. Even imagining the possibility elevated his blood pressure.

"I can see your point," his mother said, "but Jake's been your best friend since grade school. If you date Addie for any length of time, she's bound to meet him eventually. Why not get it out of the way?"

Before he could respond, his mother flashed a mischievous smile. "If it helps, I doubt he'll try to steal her from you since he's safely married now."

His jaw dropped. "Did you just make a completely inappropriate joke at my expense?"

"I suppose that depends on your definition of *inappropriate*," she said. "I love you more than anyone in the entire world, darling, but that doesn't mean I can't make fun of you."

"Just so you know, you won't be getting a card next Mother's Day."

Dimples flashed in her cheeks as she smiled, but her expression sobered a moment later. "I was kidding, of course, but seriously, how are things between you and Jake? Have you seen him lately?"

"We played racquetball together and I went over Sunday to help him screen in the back porch." Both true statements, so Giff tried to convince himself there was nothing dishonest about what he said.

His mother just watched him, the same way she had when he was a child. He'd never been able to lie to her—had never really wanted to—and he couldn't start now.

Giff caved. "He and I had a slight disagreement when I was there Sunday. About Addie. He's of the misguided opinion... Do you think I'm afraid of being alone?"

His mother looked taken aback by the question. "Most people are, to some extent, but that's not how I would describe you. You're definitely not one of those serial daters. If anything, you work too hard and forget to seek out personal relationships."

"Jake insists I'm desperate for a family." Giff's lip curled. He was a successful, well-liked man. It was galling that someone could see him as desperate in any manner. "That I only proposed to Brooke because I wanted to present you with cute grandkids."

Grace leaned back in her seat. "I always did wonder why you asked her to marry you."

"What? I thought you loved Brooke."

"I do. She's charming. But the two of you together... If she made you happy, I was prepared to be happy for the both of you. You know your father was an important man in the business community."

"Of course," Giff said, wondering what the one had to do with the other.

"He worked hard," Grace continued. "He was a good provider for us, and I loved him for that, but we fought over it, too. There were evenings he'd get wrapped up in a meeting and miss dinner, forgetting to call and let me know. But when we were at an event together and he got swept into a corner with the boys' club for wheeling and dealing, I could still feel him watching me. If I left the room, he spotted me as soon as I returned and he'd smile at me." She stopped, looking misty-eyed at the memory.

Then she gave herself a brisk shake. "I think you cared for Brooke and would have been a decent husband to her. But when she walked into a room, your eyes weren't drawn to her."

Giff remembered what he'd told Jake. "I wasn't passionate about her."

"And it's different with Addie?"

A grin broke across his face. "Much."

"Then it doesn't matter what Jake or anyone else thinks. Life is short," she said, her expression softening in a way that let him know she was still thinking of her late husband. "Follow your heart and hope for the best. That's all any of us can do."

Chapter Thirteen

After Giff had dropped his mom off and helped her carry all the suitcases inside, he found himself at loose ends. What he wanted to do was call Addie, but he knew she was at Tanner's soccer practice already. He briefly toyed with the notion of giving Jake a call, but he needed to organize his thoughts better before confronting his friend again.

Might as well get some work done. The IT people who worked for Daughtrie knew that he was looking at network security, but they didn't know he was looking at them, as well. After hours was a good time to run scans he didn't want to explain to anyone. If he was lucky, he'd find transmittal of Daughtrie's latest bids and could wrap up the whole project. He'd miss seeing Addie every day, but his tolerance for Bill Daughtrie himself was about shot. Besides, he suspected Addie would be more comfortable with their escalating romance once they were no longer in the same workplace.

The empty parking garage showed that most people had left for the day, although he spotted Robert Jenner sitting inside his red sports car, talking to a blonde Giff recognized from a different department. Giff walked quickly, not wanting a ringside seat if Jenner—unquestionably the company hound—was angling for a quickie from a coworker.

Inside the building, the office suites were eerily quiet, with minimal lights turned on and only the hum of electronic equipment to keep him company. But without the distractions of ringing phones and incoming faxes and a booming Bill Daughtrie interrupting for progress reports, Giff was able to settle in to his work and give it his full concentration.

An hour later, he was frowning, dumbfounded, at the computer screen in front of him. He'd hoped to find a recent transmittal of information and had struck out. But someone had gone into the log and deleted an action they hadn't wanted anyone else to see. Not just someone, though. According to the log-in information he unearthed, it was Addie.

He rolled the office chair back away from the desk, as if needing to put physical distance between himself and the "evidence." *It's not true.* He knew without a doubt that Addie was not the person selling out Daughtrie. Best-case scenario, she'd had a simple explanation for erasing something and she'd explain it to him when he asked.

Worst case? Someone was setting her up.

That was new. He hadn't found any red herrings on his previous e-searches. Was someone panicking because they were afraid Giff was getting close with all of his security research? Or had someone from IT hijacked the idea Addie had once brainstormed in their team meeting, to throw off suspicion by implicating someone else?

More than ever, he wished he could give her the details behind his assignment here, but Bill had required confidentiality. Giff was sworn to discretion.

Bill was antsy for the person responsible to be found and fired, so he could make an example of them and deter any future disloyalty. Giff had always wanted to expose the guilty party, as a point of professional pride. But now his motivation went much deeper—someone was jeopardizing Addie's livelihood, whether maliciously or simply because she'd been convenient somehow. Giff would not let that happen.

"EVERYTHING OKAY?" ADDIE BIT her tongue, but it was too late. The question had already escaped. Which was embarrassing, since it was the third time she'd asked since they'd been seated in the family-owned pizzeria.

And for the third time, Giff denied anything was bothering him. "I'm fine, just preoccupied with work stuff. Plus, I'm starving. Think they'll bring out our food soon?"

She fiddled with the straw in her diet soda. It was disconcerting not to believe someone whom she trusted. *Probably just a guy thing.* Weren't men known for not wanting to discuss their feelings? She just had to accept that he'd tell her whatever it was when he was ready.

She changed the subject, searching for a question that wouldn't make him feel as though he was under interrogation. "Have a nice reunion with your mom yesterday?"

His face brightened. "Yeah, I did. She can't wait to meet you. No pressure, though." He suddenly looked nervous, as if she might object to meeting the parent.

She smiled. "We'll have to get together soon."

The waitress brought out their pizza. Giff served the slices, but then sat there just looking at his in spite of having just claimed seconds ago that he was hungry.

He cleared his throat. "Quick question. I was running some scans on the network and found an anomaly in the log. Have you erased anything outgoing lately, reset anything?"

"No. I did delete some forwarded jokes from my e-mail in-box," she teased.

His mouth quirked in recognition of the joke, but he didn't quite smile. "I know you've been busy with the kids for the last couple of months, but before that, did you socialize much with the IT people? Drinks after work, karaoke on Friday, that kind of thing?"

Addie's imagination inflicted her with a mental picture of Jenner and Parnelli doing their best Hall and Oates, and she grimaced. "Definitely not."

"How well would you say you know them?"

"Not very, I guess." She was surprised by the direction of conversation, but at least he was talking now and not just brooding.

"So no Friday night poker," he surmised. "Do you know if any of them gamble?"

She stared. "Why? You looking to get a game going? Giff, no offense, but you're acting awfully weird today. Is it just because of this 'anomaly'?"

"Sorry." He spread his hands on the table, studying his fingers. "I guess I do have something on my mind that I should ask you about. I have an idea of when you could meet my mom."

"Okay," she said encouragingly, wondering if he'd

jumped topics entirely or if the two were somehow linked in his man-brain.

"I have to go to a reception this weekend. It goes without saying that I'd love for you to be my date, but…"

It clicked, then, what he wanted to ask her and maybe why he seemed so discomfited. The first time she'd ever had lunch with Giff, they'd seen his ex-fiancée and Brooke had wanted assurance that Giff wouldn't miss the upcoming wedding reception.

"The celebration for Brooke and Jake is this weekend," Addie guessed.

He looked miserable. "Yeah. It's Saturday night. I know it would probably be weird for you, meeting my mom and best friend all in one night at a party for my best friend and the woman I was supposed to have married a month ago. Plus, you have the issue of trying to find a babysitter last minute. Under other circumstances, my mom would probably volunteer, but of course, she's going. She was like Jake's second mother and—"

"Giff!"

"Yeah?"

"You're babbling." She smothered a laugh. "Which is cute but completely unnecessary. Do you want me to be there?" It wasn't only her for whom this could be weird.

"Yes." His shoulders slumped as he exhaled, looking like himself again. "Yes, I do."

"Then I'll be there. Just as I'm sure that if I had to face *my* ex and wanted to show up looking gorgeous, with a devoted date at my side, I could count on you to help me out."

He reached over and laced his fingers through hers.

"You can count on me for anything you need. And he was an idiot for letting you go."

Privately she couldn't help thinking the same thing about this Brooke woman, but that probably wasn't the right conversational opener for Saturday night.

"I HAD NO IDEA DEPARTMENT stores offered this service," Addie marveled as she pushed Nicole's stroller toward women's dresses and evening wear.

Jonna smirked. "They're getting sneaky. They know women will spend more money if they have longer to browse without tiny voices asking, 'Can we go home now?'"

Addie had called her friend immediately after lunch and the two women had agreed to meet at the mall for an emergency shopping expedition Wednesday night. When Addie had told her about Giff's asking her to the reception, Jonna had agreed to keep the kids at her house for a sleepover Saturday night; she'd also insisted that Addie needed a killer new dress. Upon arrival, they'd discovered that one of the fancier chains offered a free "drop and shop" room to their customers, where children between the ages of three and nine could play video games and create pictures with art supplies while their mothers tried on clothes. Guardians were given a pager in case the child needed anything and had to show identification to sign the kids back out.

"I can't tell you how much I appreciate your help with this," Addie said. "Not just the shopping part, but the babysitting!"

"Girl, I'm just glad you and Giff finally decided to date. If I can help make that possible, I'm more than happy to give up a single Saturday night." Her eyes glinted with humor. "Especially since Sean will be out of town this weekend. He's still planning to be at the soccer game tomorrow night, though."

"Giff told me he's looking forward to seeing me in action as the coach," Addie said. "Apparently he has a thing for sporty women."

A crease appeared between Jonna's eyebrows. "Well you're not going 'sporty' for Saturday. Try 'slinky.' Sexy. Sultry. Va-va-voom!" She pumped a fist in the air.

"Easy on the voom. This will be my introduction to his mother," Addie reminded her overzealous friend.

"Fine. Sexy but tasteful."

"And on clearance, if possible."

Jonna crossed her eyes at her. "Man are you picky."

They hit the sales racks, and fifteen minutes later Addie took a few selections into the dressing room while Jonna waited with the baby. A navy evening gown looked too matronly and a beaded white dress gaped in the bodice obviously designed for someone who could fill more than a B cup. Addie was, at best, a B minus. The red number wasn't bad, but it wasn't great, either. She huffed out a sigh and emerged into the waiting area.

"I didn't get to see any of them." Jonna pouted.

"No point in wasting your time. I'm only showing you the serious contenders. Is it petty to wish his ex wasn't quite so beautiful?"

"Yes, very." Jonna grinned.

"I'm a little nervous," Addie admitted. "Not because I'm worried about stacking up to Brooke, but…I'm not sure I'll be able to like these people. I can't even wrap my head around Giff forgiving them. The woman he wanted to marry jilted him for his best friend! How does he trust them?"

"What you're seeing as a betrayal, maybe he sees as a blessing. If she hadn't jilted him, he wouldn't be with you now."

"In that case, I should take her a bottle of champagne in thanks. Because Giff is amazing. He's good with the kids and even smarter than me about computers—"

"Only you would find that a turn-on," Jonna interrupted with an eye roll.

"And he's a fantastic kisser. I could so easily let myself fall in love with him."

"Sounds like a plan," Jonna approved. "I know Christian let you down when you tried to lean on him, but this is different. Let yourself fall. Trust Giff to catch you."

And if it didn't work out, her heart would be a giant splat on the pavement, but wasn't that the chance everyone took? At least she'd been lucky enough to meet someone worth the risk.

"ALL RIGHT, SEA TURTLES, gather 'round!" Waiting for her pint-size players to congregate, Addie winked at Tanner. From the sidelines, Jonna and Giff both gave him a thumbs-up. "I want to remind everyone that the most important things out there are to do your best and have fun. The first group in will be Mandy and Tyrone on offense, Sammy and Tanner on defense."

She couldn't help glancing apologetically in Sam's direction as she said this. The kid who'd cried throughout every practice they'd had was holding steady so far, but his eyes were red-rimmed and he was clutching a stuffed yellow bunny he insisted on carrying to the field with him. *Why not?* Addie had decided. The bunny could be their unofficial mascot. Maybe she could talk him into a stuffed turtle for the next game. She just hoped that she and Sam's parents weren't scarring the child for life by pushing him into something he wasn't ready for.

No sooner had the first quarter started than Caleb's father, predictably, got in her face, demanding to know why her kid was starting instead of his. She seriously wished she could trade Caleb and his dad to another team.

"Because he showed poor sportsmanship during warm-up, and I wasn't going to reward that kind of behavior," she said calmly. "We don't call the other team losers." *Especially when I have reason to believe they're gonna kick our butts.*

It wasn't looking good out on the field. Sammy was standing frozen in place, gripping his rabbit in front of him like a shield, and Mandy had already made a goal—for the opposite team.

"Other goal, sweetie!" Addie yelled encouragingly. "Nice kick, though." *Why in heaven's name did I agree to do this?*

But when she looked out and watched Tanner race across the grass, brow furrowed in concentration as he swept his leg toward the ball, she remembered. Tanner passed it to Tyrone, who scored—thankfully in the right goal—and Addie whooped with joy.

"Way to go, Turtles!"

By halftime, they still only had the one point, though. Giff walked over to hand Tanner his water bottle, then stayed to rub Addie's shoulders after the little boy had run off to join his friends.

"You're a natural at this," Giff told her.

"Yeah." She blew out a puff of air. "That's why we're getting slaughtered five to one. Do the kids on the Meteors team look especially tall to you? I swear they're using eight-year-old ringers."

"Ah, yes," Giff said gravely. "The seedy underbelly of community-sponsored, first grade soccer. I think I saw a news special on this."

Addie laughed, immensely cheered by his presence. "I'm glad you're here." She pressed a quick kiss to his jaw.

"Happy to help. And I mean that," he stressed. "For instance, that jerk earlier?"

She lowered her voice to an even more discreet level. "One of the team parents. My least favorite. He disagreed with a coaching decision. I took care of it."

"You sure you don't want me to rough him up?" Giff offered.

"Tempting. But probably a bad example for Tanner."

Giff returned to his seat grousing about the burden of being a good role model. Addie grinned, taking an extra moment to appreciate his retreating backside. *That man was born for jeans.*

Unfortunately, there wasn't much she could do to pass along her buoyant mood to the kids. The Sea Turtles lost by eight points, a particularly crushing defeat since it had been their first game. Despite Addie's assurance that she was proud of them for making an effort, half the team appeared to be on the verge of tears. Ironically, that didn't include Sammy.

"There's always next week," she said in the perkiest tone she could manage. "Our second game is Friday. And, remember, it's not about the scoreboard. It's about having fun."

"What's fun about losing?" Caleb demanded with a sneer.

The only replies that came immediately to mind weren't appropriate to give a six-year-old, so she dismissed everyone.

Tanner remained where he stood, scuffing his cleats in the dirt and refusing to meet her eyes.

Addie did the only thing she could think of under the circumstances. "Who's up for ice cream?"

THIRTY MINUTES LATER, Addie, Giff and Tanner were seated on garishly colored vinyl benches in an ice cream parlor decorated in chrome and neon colors. Because Sean had an early flight tomorrow, he and Jonna had elected not to join them. Tanner sat next to Giff, spooning his way through a banana split. He had chocolate syrup, strawberry sauce and whipped cream smeared across his chin and upper lip.

Addie smiled at the picture he made. "Feel better now, honey?"

"Yeah." Tanner looked up with a frown. "But our team stinks, Aunt Addie."

His words struck her as failure. She obviously wasn't getting the message across that winning wasn't everything; the last thing she wanted was to raise a kid like Caleb. She opened her mouth to object to Tanner's statement, but Giff caught her eye, subtly signaling to himself with his index finger.

Addie sat back, interested to hear how he would address this.

"The important thing isn't who can kick the farthest or run the fastest," he said sternly. "It's that you are part of a team, and you should appreciate having one. It's a special privilege."

Tanner straightened, looking surprised by his idol's disappointed tone. "But—"

"I used to play football," Giff said. "And I don't remember how many games we won or lost, but I know the names of all my teammates. They were my friends, some of my best friends. And I miss them. When you're a grown-up, you don't always get that kind of support, people who have your back and celebrate your victories with you. If you think your team should be doing better, it's your responsibility to help them get better, to encourage them and train hard with them. Can you do that?"

Tanner swallowed. "Yes, sir."

"Good." Giff tousled the boy's hair and smiled. "Then go ahead and finish your ice cream before it melts. Tomorrow's a school day."

Addie sat back, impressed. There were probably a number of men who would be able to fulfill the comparatively easy role of buddy for fun outings like fishing trips and baseball, but it took skill to also be a disciplinarian, one who made his point without yelling or overreacting.

In the background, Elvis gave way to the Beach Boys on the brightly lit jukebox. Nicole, seeming to like the beat, bicycled her chubby legs. Tanner pushed his empty plastic bowl away from the edge of the table.

"Mr. Giff?"

"Yeah, sport?"

"I'll try next week to do like you said, to be a better teammate," the boy said firmly. "Will you come watch?"

"I'd be honored to."

Out in the parking lot, Giff walked Addie and the kids to her car.

She bumped his shoulder with hers. "You rocked in there, by the way. Is there anything you're not good at?"

"Shockingly, yes." He pulled a face, looking a lot like Tanner whenever he was asked to eat broccoli. "I'm the world's worst dancer, as you'll probably see for yourself Saturday. I have no rhythm, two left feet. It's tragic, really. I hate dancing."

"Can't we just stand on the dance floor with our arms around each other?" She placed Nicole into her car seat while Tanner buckled himself in next to his sister. Then she shut the door. "Here, I'll show you."

She twined her arms around Giff's neck, letting herself melt against him so that nothing separated their bodies except for a few articles of clothing. Her breathing quickened.

He trailed his fingers over the nape of her neck. "Like this?"

"We're supposed to sway a little," she murmured, demonstrating. Her hips brushed across his, the whisper of friction enough to suffuse her body with heat. "But yeah, this is the basic idea."

"Huh." He stopped, his expression mystified. "Turns out, I love dancing."

As soon as Giff heard the footsteps outside his office Friday evening, he realized he'd made a tactical error. He'd stayed late, after everyone else had left, because he was determined to unravel the electronic signature on the altered log. But he'd pushed his luck. He'd been able to avoid Bill for the past couple of days because the man was on-site, visiting the location of one of their bigger projects. Apparently, the man had decided to stop back by the office before officially starting his weekend.

"Was hoping to find you here, son."

Giff stood hastily. "Actually, I was just leaving."

The man beetled his brows. "You haven't even shut down your computer. What's the hurry? I'm paying you good money and I deserve a report on your progress. Or maybe that's the problem? You're afraid to talk to me because you still haven't made any and you know a few words from me could damage your professional reputation."

Giff gritted his teeth and reined in his temper for Addie's sake. "Actually, I have made progress this week. I have a new lead, but so far it's inconclusive." He was obligated to give Bill the information; all he could do now was damage control.

"How do you mean? I'm expecting to hear from Groverton first thing on Monday. Did the bid get leaked or not?"

"There's no evidence of that, specifically. But someone altered the system log."

"And we don't have a way to find out who that someone was? Which computer it was done from?"

"The specific terminal wouldn't matter. All the computers in the office are networked together. A person would just have to log in with their password. And Addie Caine's password was used for this deletion."

Bill clapped his meaty hands together. "I knew it! I told you, didn't I, that it would be one of those women?"

You sexist ass. "This doesn't prove she's guilty. It suggests to me that someone hacked her information or otherwise had access to her password and user ID. Addie herself suggested something like this in a team meeting a couple of weeks ago, redirecting blame to someone else. Someone's using her own idea against her."

"Or she knew that making the suggestion would lead you to believe that. Are you really that naive, Baker, or are you prolonging this because of your own ulterior motives where that little redhead is concerned?"

Giff's jaw clenched. He badly wanted to tell Bill to shove it, but then he would lose access to any possibility of clearing Addie. "Just give me a week," he said recklessly. "I'll find out who did this even if I have to work around the clock. I swear."

"All right." The man's gaze was steely. "You've got until this time next Friday and not a second more."

Chapter Fourteen

Addie dubiously eyed the dress that hung from the top of her bedroom door. If she chickened out of wearing it, would Jonna somehow be able to psychically sense it?

"Are you sure about this?" Addie had asked her friend in the department store dressing room.

"Please, it's Fashion 101. You've heard the cleavage or legs rule."

Addie had laughed. "Cleavage, not so much an option."

"That's why this little number is perfect for you. And I mean that in a good way."

With her best friend egging her on, Addie had chosen a short-sleeved turtleneck dress in deep, dark green. At night, it would look black from a distance. The silky material was shot through with randomly placed iridescent threads meant to catch the light and the eye. Her hesitation over the dress hadn't been the way it hugged the curve of her hip, it had been the length of the skirt.

"You're forgetting, I have to meet his mother in this," she'd nearly shrieked.

Jonna had rolled her eyes. "It's not that short. It's simply outside of your normal comfort zone. Just don't bend over at the party, and you'll be fine. Plus, I saw a great pair of kitten heels on sale that would look great with that color."

Now, alone in the unnaturally quiet apartment, Addie hoped her friend knew what she was talking about. Jonna had shown up twenty minutes ago to pick up the kids. Tanner had been vibrating with excitement over a promised *Star Wars* DVD marathon.

She plugged in two different curling irons to heat up while she applied light, shimmery makeup, then zipped herself into the dress. Instead of fighting her curls tonight, she styled her hair in profusion of them. She stepped into the new heels and was just sliding in a pair of slim dangling gold earrings when the doorbell rang.

Here goes nothing.

Addie made a point of looking through the peephole first before she remembered that Tanner wasn't here to witness her good example. Smiling to herself, she opened the door. Giff stood on the other side of the threshold with flowers. He looked like James Bond's hot younger brother in his black suit.

"Wow," Giff said. "My only regret is that I didn't get to watch you walk to the door. You look incredible."

Thank you, Jonna. "Back atcha."

"These are for you." He held out a simple arrangement of about half a dozen peach roses; secured around the base of the flowers was a small stuffed bear holding a soccer ball and wearing a green jersey that read Coach.

"That's perfect," Addie declared. In her heels, it was easier than ever to reach up and meet his lips. She pulled back, taking the flowers to put in water. "If we kept doing that, I'd have to redo my hair and makeup."

"If we kept doing that, we could skip the reception altogether," he suggested with a grin.

She took a deep breath. "That is officially the most enticing idea I've ever heard in my life. But people would miss you."

He brushed his knuckles over her cheek. "Rain check?"

"Definitely."

THE HOTEL THAT JAKE AND BROOKE had chosen for their reception was well-known for its prestigious social events. Frankly, it was a little intimidating in its splendor. Addie realized that Giff was used to places like this; she was not.

"Have you ever been here before?" Giff asked her after the valet had helped her out of the car.

"No, but I've heard of it. Isn't this where they have the annual Midsummer Night Gala?"

"Yep. This way," he said, dropping his free hand to the small of her back. In the other, he carried a silver-wrapped gift box.

They passed a sign for the McBride Reception and followed the corridor to a ballroom. A uniformed hotel employee was politely checking invitations. They'd barely stepped foot inside and set their present on the appropriate side table when Giff asked if she saw where the bar had been set up.

Addie snickered. "Desperate for a drink?"

"No, I just thought it would be nice to get you a

glass of wine before we're accosted." He groaned. "Too late."

"Giff!"

"Hope you weren't thirsty," he muttered near Addie's ear. "We're not going anywhere for a while."

Addie followed his gaze to a stunning woman who had thick white hair and a feminine variation of Giff's smile.

"Mom." Placing one arm around the woman, Giff leaned in to kiss her on the cheek. "What were you doing, lying in wait for our arrival?"

Instead of responding directly to him, the woman turned to Addie with a comically pained expression. "Please forgive my incredibly rude son—clearly, I went wrong somewhere. What he meant to say was that he's delighted to see me and that I'm Grace Baker. You must be Addie."

"Addie Caine." She shook hands with Grace. "And it's a real pleasure to meet you."

"Why don't you come with me and we'll get you a drink, dear? With manners like this one has, we dare not leave it up to him," Grace chirped.

"Hey!" Giff objected.

Addie laughed. "A glass of white wine would be lovely. Lead the way."

The three of them navigated an impressive crowd. Between the partygoers and the tuxedoed waitstaff circulating with glasses of champagne and bringing out trenchers of dressing for the soon-to-be-served salad course, Addie felt more claustrophobic here in the grand ballroom than she did in her office building's elevator.

"This is a lot of well-wishers," she said, squeezing

to the side so that a couple of broad-shouldered men could pass.

"With Jake being a fireman, they invited everyone from his station," Giff explained. "And any of his army buddies who happened to be stateside. Not to mention a newspaper staff and both of their families. Mom, do you know where the guests of honor are?"

Grace pointed to the far corner of the room where a photographer had set up a backdrop. Brooke, glowing in a white beaded evening gown, was currently having her portrait made with two petite blondes who looked enough alike that they had to be related. Addie guessed that the handsome man with close-cropped hair and adoring expression who stood watching them from a few feet was probably Jake.

"Is that him?" she asked softly. "Your friend?"

He nodded. "Jake McBride, the one and only."

"He's good-looking," she remarked, studying the man with detached curiosity. He'd played such a pivotal role in Giff's life that she'd wondered what he would be like.

Giff started to stiffen at her side, but caught himself. His contrite smile was endearingly self-aware. "It's possible I've developed a complex about my friend."

In front of them, Grace clucked her tongue. "Really, dear. There's nothing less attractive than an insecure man."

Addie tilted her head toward Giff and whispered, "You couldn't be unattractive if you tried."

"You're very good for my ego," he whispered back. "I plan on keeping you around."

They reached the bar and got their round of drinks.

Grace fished the olive out of her martini and raised the glass as if toasting Addie. "So tell me about how the two of you met."

Addie almost groaned at the recollection of how discombobulated she'd been that day. It was not a flattering memory. Then again, there was something liberating in knowing he'd already seen her at her worst and wanted her anyway.

"It was through work," Giff said, a smile lurking in his voice as if he had easily guessed the direction of Addie's thoughts. "She was in the office break room and made an immediate, unmistakable impression on me."

Addie considered discreetly stepping on his toe.

"It must be interesting to work with the person you're dating. Giff, how much longer will this assignment be?"

Giff's expression turned inscrutable and he sipped his imported beer. Addie had the fleeting impression that he was stalling before answering.

"Grace Baker, is that you?" A woman dripping diamonds and sporting a hair color unknown to Mother Nature exited the line at the bar to hug Giff's mother. "Why, I haven't seen you in a month of Sundays. Where have you been hiding?"

As the two friends, who were apparently acquainted through bridge club, began chatting, Giff led Addie away through the crowd.

"We'll catch up with Mom later," Giff predicted. "She asked me if you had any pictures of the kids with you."

Addie's cheeks warmed, patting the slim formal purse

she carried. "Actually, I do. They haven't been with me two full months, and I've already become one of those people. By October, friends won't be able to visit me without being forced to sit through home movies of Tanner's soccer games. Promise you'll talk some sense into me if I get that bad?"

He laughed. "Can't. Who do you think will be making the popcorn while you cue up the soccer footage?"

She grinned, easily able to envision that. "Speaking of the kids, do you mind if I step outside the ballroom and look for a quiet corner to call them? This is the first time Tanner's spent the night away from me and I just wanted to check in with him before we sit down to dinner, before he falls asleep."

He kissed the top of her head. "Tell him I said hi. I'll be over there." He pointed to a cluster of men not far from the gift table. "There are some people I wanted to talk to about post-Daughtrie projects for the winter."

Addie threaded her way between the round tables set for dinner, each boasting a tropical centerpiece of orchids and anthuriums. Small bags of candied macadamia nuts had been placed at each setting as party favors. Giff had told her the bride and groom were married in Hawaii; they were obviously trying to recapture a bit of that magic for their celebration.

The hallway seemed bizarrely subdued after the buzz of activity in the ballroom, and Addie was glad to find that she could get a signal.

Jonna answered on the first ring. No doubt she'd anticipated her friend's call. "He loved the dress, am I right?"

"You were right. And I met his mother, who didn't

seem scandalized, so I guess the skirt's really not that short."

"Was she nice," Jonna asked, "or one of those stand-offish types who thinks no woman is good enough for her son?"

"She was great. Made jokes, treated me warmly, wants to hear all about the kids. I swear, Jonna, every detail about being involved with Giff is too good to be true. I almost feel like I should be worried."

When she was a kid, she used to have these great dreams where she could fly. It was her favorite child-hood fantasy and she'd loved those dreams…but there'd always been the inescapable knowledge nagging at her, that it wasn't real and that she'd have to wake up sooner or later.

"Then you're an idiot," Jonna said with affectionate disdain. "Get back in that party, enjoy the expensive catering and have the time of your life with the hot guy who seems crazy about you."

"In a minute," Addie promised. "Can I talk to Tanner first?"

After her nephew assured her that he was having a wonderful time being spoiled rotten for the evening at Jonna's, Addie told him good-night and flipped her phone closed. She headed back into the ballroom, paus-ing in the doorway to orient herself and see if the group of businessmen were in the same place as when she'd left.

As if her presence were a tangible thing, like a shock of electricity, Giff stopped in midsentence and lifted his head. Across the crowded room, his gaze locked with hers and he smiled.

ON STAGE AT THE FRONT of the ballroom, one of the waiters spoke into a microphone, informing them that they should all take their seats and dinner would be served momentarily. Giff braced himself, wondering what to expect from the group dynamic at his table. Even though Brooke and Jake hadn't used a bridal party at their wedding, the seating arrangements treated Giff as best man and Brooke's sister, Meg, as the maid of honor. The head table would be the happy couple, Giff and Addie, plus the wildly unconventional Meg. Her date for the evening had been a tattoo artist who'd stormed out moments ago after an argument with Meg. The meal should be…interesting.

He placed a hand on the curve of Addie's hip, trying to keep his eyes from wandering down to the hem of her killer dress and the shapely legs revealed below. "It's not too late. I think I saw a couple of unclaimed seats back there. We could be the Holdensteins at Table 14."

Addie smirked at him over her shoulder. "They're the guests of honor, Giff. You can't avoid them all night."

"I haven't been avoiding them," he protested. "They've been surrounded by people ever since we got here and I was patiently biding my time, knowing I'd have the chance to offer my congratulations at dinner."

"Not from Table 14 you wouldn't."

He traced his fingers up her back, appreciating the silky softness of her dress but knowing intuitively that her skin would be softer. "What if I said the reason I hadn't gone out of my way to introduce you to them was because I've been enjoying your company so much this evening that I selfishly wanted to keep you all to myself?"

"I'd say you were very suave." Her gray eyes sparkled. "And very full of it."

And with that, he was converted. Suddenly he couldn't wait for Jake to meet her because even his skeptical, overprotective friend would have to see how sexy and witty she was. *There's no chance I want Addie just because she could be a good wife and mother. I want Addie because she's Addie.*

But just as Jake had underestimated Giff, Giff had underestimated his friends. Had he really been worried about tension? Brooke and Jake went out of their way to greet Addie with friendly—but not intimidating—enthusiasm.

"I'm so glad Giff brought you tonight," Brooke said with a welcoming smile. "I had a good feeling about you from the moment I saw you at the bistro. Woman's intuition."

Meg snorted, peering around her sister to where Addie sat between Jake and Giff. "Intuition, ha! Don't let her fool you. Up until a few months ago, my sister believed solely in facts and figures and had no use for stuff like instinct and emotion."

Brooke didn't even bother getting defensive. Instead, she simply shrugged. "I've changed for the better."

You're not the only one, Giff thought. When he'd been talking to those businessmen earlier, he'd realized that he was no longer as mindlessly driven as he used to be. He was still interested in what was going on in Houston's business community, but he had other priorities now, too. He could see himself getting just as emotionally invested in one of Tanner's soccer games as local technology mergers.

He used to be the kind of man that got husbands in trouble, monopolizing their time at social events with industry discussions until their wives complained. Tonight, he'd been the one fidgeting, looking for the soonest opportunity to excuse himself from the conversation. Of course, a shift in priorities wasn't the only reason he'd been restless this evening.

People asked about what he was doing these days which turned the topic to his network forensics for Daughtrie. Even though no one had asked about—or even knew about—his investigative attempts there, the situation and Bill Daughtrie's ultimatum were weighing heavily on Giff's mind. He'd never felt guilty before about not being able to tell Addie the whole purpose for his being hired because confidentiality had always been part of his job. He was used to keeping client secrets; that was simply professionalism. As someone who worked in the field, she would understand.

However, now that he'd discovered she was being targeted, used, it was difficult to remember this was a professional matter. It felt damn personal. He wanted to confide in her at the same time he wanted to shield her from it until he had more answers.

"Yo, Baker." Despite his attempt to sound glib, there was an undercurrent of concern in Jake's voice. "You still with us?"

"Sorry. My mind wandered." He wondered if Jake and Brooke, based on past experience with him, would assume work had preoccupied his thoughts. Ironic that they would be right and completely wrong at the same time.

"Giff, have you seen the wedding cake yet?" Brooke

asked out of nowhere. "Jake, you should show him. We have a few minutes before the next course, you two take your time."

Jake flashed a wide cowboy grin at his wife. "Darlin', you know I love you, but subtle you ain't. You might as well have told us to take a hike."

Giff could feel the vibration of the laugh Addie smothered, and he exchanged grins with her.

"Subtle is for people who have more patience," Brooke said, adopting an aggravated tone. "Now go show your friend the darn cake."

"Yes, ma'am." Jake rose from his chair. "Giff, you might as well come with me. She's not going to let us eat until we've talked."

Even though both men knew the cake had been nothing but a hastily seized excuse for giving them a moment's privacy, they meandered in that direction. Next to the stage, set up for the band to play after dinner, was a white lattice-work archway. Underneath, a chocolate groom's cake and four-tiered wedding cake sat on a decorated table. Giff grinned at the unique cake toppers—a plastic red fireman's hat and a tiny typewriter.

"Cute," he remarked.

"I'm sorry about what I said to you at the house," Jake said without preamble. "Brooke about wrung my neck when she heard what happened. She's worried that's why you're quiet tonight, that you're ticked. All I can say is, my intentions were good."

"Understood. You were looking out for a buddy. Which is sometimes annoying as all hell, but it's part of being a team." Giff recalled the lecture he'd given to Tanner in the ice cream parlor. Teammates weren't perfect, but they supported one another anyway.

"If it makes you feel better, I'm eating crow tonight. Addie's wonderful."

"I know. Stay away from her," Giff said in a mock growl.

"I can't do that. I know all kinds of great stories about you that I bet she'll want to hear." Whistling softly, Jake sauntered back toward the table.

Making good on his threat, Jake entertained everyone over roast beef with embellished stories of Giff's adolescent scrapes. But Giff was happy to pay him back in kind, regaling them with Jake's many misadventures. Meg finally pleaded with them to stop because she was laughing so hard her eyes were tearing up.

"If I lose a contact, one of you is going to have to drive me home," she said.

When they realized that the tables around them were being cleared, conversation slowed and they got down to the serious business of finishing their food. Except that Giff noticed Addie was pushing the roasted rosemary potatoes around her plate without actually eating any of them.

He leaned close so that no one could hear them. And because he enjoyed the excuse to breathe in her scent. "You okay? You're not uncomfortable with Jake and Brooke?" He'd been impressed with how well the evening was going, but maybe that was because he was already well acquainted with everyone at the table. It might be different for Addie, as an outsider to the group.

But she looked stunned by his question. "They're

terrific. I wasn't honestly sure I could like them, but I was wrong. In fact…Jake reminds me a lot of my big brother. You would have liked Zach. I'm sorry you'll never get to meet him."

"I feel like I already have," Giff said, "through his kids."

She gave him a tremulous smile. "I love you."

Giff's heart stopped. That admission had been the last thing he expected and until he'd heard it aloud he hadn't realized just how much he would love hearing it. His lips parted, the natural response on the tip of his tongue. But the guilt he'd been feeling earlier, over not being able to tell her the whole truth about what was going on in her department, tripped him up. Wouldn't it be better, when he told her he loved her for the first time, for there to be no secrets between them?

"I—"

She shook her head, placing a finger on his lips. "It's okay, you don't have to say it. That was… It's too soon. This was the wrong place."

"No! No, I'm glad you said it. I feel the same way."

Biting her lip, she regarded him with equal parts doubt and optimism. Conflicted over what else to say, he simply squeezed her hand and hoped that his feelings spoke for themselves.

After dinner was officially over, Jake's father went to the front of the room to thank everyone for attending and sharing in the newlyweds' joy. Then he made a toast, followed by Brooke's dad and Meg, who delivered a passage in French that sounded elegant but which she admitted to her table had actually been an extremely naughty poem. Giff realized that, as informal best man, he was expected to say something, as well.

He cleared his throat. "I'm Giff Baker and I've known Jake pretty much my entire life. We grew up together, played football together, and drank entirely too much beer at the Dixie Chicken together."

Mention of the landmark bar in College Station was met with hoots and a smattering of applause.

"But even if I'd only met Jake today," Giff continued, "I could tell at a glance that he's married to exactly the woman he was meant to be with, the beautiful Brooke McBride. Jake, Brooke, trust me when I tell you, I couldn't be happier that the two of you found each other and ended up together." He winked at Addie, then hoisted his glass to the room in general. "Cheers."

On the heels of Giff's toast, the band began to play. Couples straggled onto the portable parquet dance floor.

Meg scooted her chair back and smiled at Giff. "I don't know if you noticed, but my date eighty-sixed me pretty early in the evening. Addie, would you mind if I borrowed Giff for a quick turn around the floor?"

"Uh, would you settle for me instead?" Jake interrupted. "Giff hates dancing."

Addie giggled, drawing curious gazes from around their table.

Giff recalled holding her in the orange glow beneath the ice cream parlor's parking lot lights; the urge to have her in his arms again was overwhelming. "Actually, I very recently discovered I do enjoy dancing. But I'm afraid all of my dances are promised to someone else tonight." He held his hand out to Addie.

As they walked away from the table, Meg's voice followed them. "Lordy, those two are almost as sappy as you guys."

It wasn't until they'd reached the edge of the dance floor that Giff frowned. "I'm not sure I thought this through."

"What's the matter?"

"All the stuff we discussed before," he reminded her wryly. "Two left feet, lack of rhythm, coordination more suited to the end zone than the fox-trot. I liked the slow dancing, but this song is a little fast for what I had in mind."

She brightened. "Oh, I can fix that. Just give me a second."

Addie let go of his hand and made a beeline for the bandstand. The pop song faded out—a verse sooner than Giff had anticipated—and a poignant ballad replaced it. She sashayed back to Giff wearing a self-satisfied smile.

"I told them the bride specifically requested something slow and romantic," she explained.

He laughed, then pulled her into his arms, kissing her before they began their obligatory swaying to the music. The material of her dress rustled against his clothes in a soft, intimate swish, and he tightened his hold on her. She was a perfect fit for him. But as much as he was enjoying her tantalizing nearness, it only left him wanting more. He ached to be closer, to be inside her.

He captured her gaze with his, trying to see if she felt the same way. "Addie."

"We could go back to my place," she offered shyly. "The kids aren't there."

His pulse quickened; she *was* experiencing the same need that pounded through him.

"Or we could go to mine. You've never seen my house." He wanted to share it with her, wanted to share all of himself. Smiling, he touched his forehead to hers. "Plus, I live closer."

"Then what are we still doing here?"

THERE WAS A LOT TO ADMIRE about Giff's house. But as Addie preceded him inside she found herself thinking not about the spacious Spanish tiled kitchen or high graceful ceilings or the backyard pool and hot tub that were visible through the Palladian window—but about underwear.

When she'd been getting dressed for this evening, she'd entertained the ideas of various body-enhancing options for beneath her daring dress. A padded bra, perhaps, for her top half or a high-waisted minimizer for the bottom. Now, she was vastly grateful she'd passed on those in favor of a simple set of pale green bra and panties edged in emerald lace.

Giff loosened his tie. "Can I get you anything to drink?"

"Thanks, but I'm good." Her eyes were riveted to his hands, watching as he removed the tie and tossed it over the back of a kitchen chair, atop the jacket he'd carried inside. There was no reason for her throat to have gone dry, except she couldn't help the progression of her thoughts from that innocuous accessory to other articles of clothing. Images tumbled through her mind, her undressing Giff, Giff undressing her. Touching her.

She swallowed. "On second thought, I could use a glass of water."

He was chivalrous enough not to comment on her change of heart. "Coming right up."

Still finding it difficult to look away from him, she ignored her surroundings and followed him with her gaze as he opened a cabinet and pulled down a glass. He filled it with filtered water from the refrigerator and carried it back to her.

Their fingers met as he passed it to her. "Here you go."

She drank some gratefully, then smiled. "Nice and cool. Thank you. It was getting hot in here."

He removed the glass from her hand and set it on the counter behind her. The house, dark beyond the kitchen, was silent except for a loudly ticking clock in the next room that could have just as well been her heart.

Giff's voice was a low rumble as he wrapped his arms around her. "Would you like the grand tour now?"

She shook her head, her body so sensitized by his nearness that even the brush of her hair across her neck made her shiver. "Later." *Much later.*

He dipped his head toward her and their mouths fused in a hot, open kiss. Their tongues slid together, and she caught his bottom lip gently between her teeth. Giff's hands had dropped to her waist. She was almost surprised to find her own hands clutching his shirtfront.

With shaking fingers, she attempted to unbutton it, but was distracted by the increasing urgency of their kisses and quit. He rocked her pliant body against his hardness, and she moaned, immediately repeating the action. His hands slid up her back and she heard the soft rasp of tiny metallic teeth. Cool air hit her bared skin, and his fingers edged beneath the material. Then her dress pooled at her feet.

"God bless whoever invented zippers," Giff said reverently. He hissed in a breath. "Damn, you're beautiful."

She peered up at him. "Thank you. But I feel underdressed."

He shrugged out of his shirt in record time, then his belt hit the tile floor. "I know we postponed the tour, but would you like to see my bedroom?"

"I thought you'd never ask." Emboldened by the way he was devouring her with his gaze, she walked ahead of him into the shadowed living room, adding a swing to her hips as she passed.

"You're evil," he drawled. "Turns out, I like that in a woman."

She shot him a grin over her shoulder. "I just realized I don't know where I'm going."

"Doesn't matter. I'd follow you anywhere." He advanced on her, grabbing her around the waist. In one fluid motion, he lifted her off the ground and spun her toward the couch. They landed with her in his lap, kissing once again.

Giff drew his teeth along the sensitive curve of her neck, palming one breast through the silky material of her bra. "We may not make it to the bed."

Her body melted at the raw need in his voice, and she arched into his touch. "Keep doing that and I promise I won't complain."

When he reached for the front clasp of her bra, she could feel the slight tremble in his touch and tenderness rushed through her.

"I know it sounds like a line," he whispered, "but I don't think I've ever wanted a woman this badly."

She skimmed her hands over the muscled planes of his chest. "I'm inclined to believe you, since I've never wanted anyone this badly, either."

Truthfully, she was surprised by the straightforward intensity of her feelings. Addie had only taken a few lovers in her life and it had been years since she'd been with someone new. She might have expected some momentary awkwardness between them, or shyness over Giff's seeing her nude body for the first time, but as he slid her bra away, leaving her bared to his touch, all she felt was a deep, delicious sense of expectation pulsing through her.

Watching her face, he thumbed the peak of her breast and she met his gaze, reveling in the way he touched her, relishing the power she found in touching him, until the escalating sensations became unbearable. She squeezed her eyes shut and threw her head back, rocking against him.

It felt so good.

But when Giff pulled her astride him and finally thrust inside her, *that* felt incredible. With one hand cupping her hip, he helped her keep her balance as she raised herself up and moved against him. She knew from working with Giff that he was a focused, goal-oriented man, and now she was the recipient of his thorough, determined finesse. He subtly slowed her down when she would have pushed harder, prolonging the ripples of pleasure until they built into waves that threatened to crash over her. Then he slid a hand down to where they were joined, matching his caress to the pace of their bodies.

Addie quivered, then screamed. She felt like an elastic band that had stretched beyond its capacity and snapped, shooting out into the cosmos. Giff surged up into her, his embrace tightening as his fingers splayed over her spine. Then they both collapsed against the back of the couch, her head resting on his shoulder.

He trailed a hand over her hair. "Addie."

She tilted her head just enough that he could see her sleepy smile. "You lied to me."

"What?" His muscles bunched beneath her hands.

"You definitely do *not* have a problem with rhythm."

Chapter Fifteen

Giff got to the office around 9 a.m. on Monday morning, a definite spring in his step as he crossed the parking garage. After he and Addie had kept each other awake into the wee hours of Saturday night, he'd hated to let her go yesterday morning. She'd had to pick up the kids, though, and he hadn't wanted to intrude on the Caines' Sunday together.

As his mother might have teasingly advised, *"Really, dear, there's nothing less attractive than a needy man."* So Giff had met his mother for Sunday brunch instead, his way of apologizing for the fact that he and Addie had ducked out of the reception without spending any more time with Grace. His mother had forgiven him with a sly smile.

"Well, I suppose it's my own fault. I did tell you that you should be passionate about something in your life besides work. But you have to bring Addie around sometime soon. And I want to meet those adorable children I've been hearing so much about."

"Don't worry, Mom. I plan on their being around a lot."

Now, as Giff punched the button to call the elevator,

he wondered how Addie would feel about his inviting Grace to Friday night's soccer game. He stepped inside the elevator in such a good mood that he found himself whistling along to the former rock song that had been cruelly transformed into lifeless, instrumental background music. There was a ding when he reached the seventh floor and the doors parted.

Addie! His senses automatically registered her unexpected presence directly in front of him and his joy at seeing her. It took a second later for his intellect to catch up, for him to realize that she was holding a white cardboard box and that her gray eyes were swimming with tears.

"Addie, what—"

"You SOB," she grated. "Don't speak to me."

"What?" After the weekend they'd shared? He'd told her he loved her! Or, implied it, anyway. "I don't…" Except that, suddenly, he did. *Bill.*

Panic seized Giff, clogging his throat. He sounded as if he were choking on rusty nails when he offered the only words that sprang to mind—possibly the worst thing any man could say in circumstances like these. "I can explain."

"Get out of the elevator!" she ordered, her voice harsh.

He stepped into the office suite but tried to prevent her from entering. They had to talk about this, he couldn't just let her go when she was this upset. Once out of the elevator, he realized that both Gabi Lopez and Pepper Harrington were hovering in the background. Gabi looked upset and unsure, wringing her hands. Pepper stood warriorlike with her hands on her hips, glaring at him as if she were trying to incinerate him with laser beam eyes.

The second he'd taken to study the other two women had given Addie the advantage. She'd moved fast for someone in high-heeled boots. She hit the down arrow before the doors had fully closed, then used the box like a shield, blocking him from getting anywhere near her while she turned sideways and boarded the elevator.

"Add—"

Her silent, betrayed face disappeared behind the metal doors. He stood dumbfounded for heartbeats of time that felt like entire eras dragging by, then whirled around.

"You!" He jabbed an index finger at Pepper. "What the hell happened here?"

"Bill fired her," the brunette informed him icily. "Thanks to you, apparently."

No. Oh, God, no. She must hate him. What had Bill been thinking? Giff had explained to the man....

If he took the stairs, he might have a chance at catching up to her. He dove for the stairwell. He was lucky that in his rush, he didn't fall and break his neck on the concrete steps. Although he couldn't imagine that doing so would be any more painful than the jagged accusation in Addie's tear-filled eyes.

The exit door burst open with a clang that reverberated through the entire parking garage. "Wait! Addie, it's not what you think." He sprinted toward her.

She was standing by her car, trying unsuccessfully to get one of the back doors open. "I don't know *what* to think. Less than forty-eight hours ago, I told some man that I loved him and then we spent all Saturday night and most of Sunday morning... I knew we had sex, Giff. I didn't know I was getting screwed."

He flinched. "Whatever Bill told you, it's not true."

She dropped the box of belongings with a thud. "He said he hired you because someone was stealing proprietary information and selling it to a rival, losing us jobs. Fact?"

"Yes, but—"

"And that the whole time you were working on network changes with us, you'd also been instructed to 'get to know us better.'" She made air-quotes, the ugly innuendo dripping from her words like corrosive acid.

He clenched his fists at his sides, unfamiliar helplessness mingled with rage that she'd been hurt. "No, Addie, that has nothing to do with us. You—"

"Really? Because I seem to recall you asking me bizarrely out of place questions about how well I knew my coworkers. Considering how little dirt I had to share, I'm surprised you didn't drop me then and there and take Pepper out Saturday instead."

"Damn it, Addie, stop. Please." Saturday had been special. "It wasn't like that. You know it isn't."

Fury flared in her eyes, but it self-extinguished, leaving her looking confused and defeated. "Bill told me you brought him evidence against me."

"He said I had until this Friday, I never—"

"You were going to string me along for another week?" She finally fumbled open the back door of her car and shoved the box inside so viciously that it slid off the seat into the floor. Giff heard something break.

"If you would just hear me out, Addie, I promise—"

"That what? That I won't be sorry? I've *been* hearing you out. Against my better judgment at times, and this is where it landed me." She opened the driver side door. "You know, you and Jonna talk about Christian like he's a jerk because he left me, but at least he was honest about what he was doing. You lied! You knew I didn't want to get involved, you wore me down, and you were exploiting me the whole time. So, no. I don't think I'm going to be listening to you anymore, Giff."

She climbed into the car and slammed the door so hard he wouldn't have been surprised if the windows had shattered. Or if a wheel had fallen off. She revved the motor and, not entirely sure what she was capable of when she was this angry, he took several large steps back, prepared to duck behind a concrete pillar if necessary.

Watching her go felt like having his heart clawed out of his chest. He was in actual physical pain, so much so that it was hard to think. *Get it together.* He had to focus, had to come up with a plan of action. Somehow he had to win Addie back; he had to find a way to clear her name. And somewhere along the way, he might also try to squeeze in time to drop Bill Daughtrie out a seventh-story window.

"WHAT THE HELL DO YOU THINK you're doing?" There was a part of Giff that was advising him to dial it down, a rational part that recognized Daughtrie having security escort him from the premises wasn't going to help Addie in the long run. But Giff could barely hear that small reasonable part of him over the instincts that were clamoring for vengeance, that wanted to howl because Addie had been misused.

And blamed him for it.

Bill half rose from his chair, planting his palms on the edge of his desk. "What I think I'm doing is running my company, son. *My* company. I heard from Groverton before I even got to the office this morning. We were underbid, and I decided to put an end to this bull. You've worked up the security improvements, I've seen the recommendations. Let's go ahead and put them in place now. I got rid of the leak."

"Addie was not the leak!"

"And did you come to that decision using your…" Bill twisted his lips in an ugly sneer "…brain?"

"It's not her," Giff repeated flatly.

Bill reclined back in his chair. "You don't know that. The only shred of evidence you've managed to pin down so far points to her. But even if you were right—and you're not—my problem is taken care of. With the new security measures in place, it will be a damn sight harder for anyone to pull this again. And their scapegoat is gone. Implicating Addie was a one-shot deal and I called their bluff. If it happens going forward, then we'll know instantly it wasn't her and more heads roll."

You bastard. Bill didn't truly believe she was guilty, he just wanted an expedient solution.

"And you're not worried about a wrongful termination suit?" Giff would gladly offer his testimony as an expert witness.

Bill rolled his eyes. "I was well within my rights to fire a suspicious employee. One, I might add, who has missed a slew of time in the past two months and whose professionalism has been called into question of late. I'd like to see her try to scrounge up the money to take on me and my lawyers. Now, if that's all, why don't you get out of my office?"

Giff tried to see his way through the red haze to a solution. Appealing to Bill's better nature was out; the man clearly didn't have one. So how could Giff use the man's baser nature to manipulate him?

He took a deep breath. "You told me I had until Friday to investigate this."

"I invoked my right to change my mind," Bill said in a bored tone. "It's my company. What aren't you understanding about that?"

"I'd like to make you an offer. Give me until Friday, and I'll give you back every penny you gave me to do this job." Giff saw the light of greed dawn in the man's eyes and knew he had him. After all, Giff's salary had not been insubstantial. And with some of the recently lost jobs, Daughtrie was starting to feel the financial pinch.

"Maybe I won't find anything," Giff said, "in which case nothing changes for you except that you get that big fat refund. But what if Addie really wasn't behind this? That means you still have someone here in this company cheating you, *laughing* at you. Wouldn't you want the chance to toss him out on his ass?"

Bill's eyes narrowed to slits. "Until Friday," he agreed. "But you start activating the new security protocols now. We're not giving anyone the chance to do this again."

Because he couldn't bring himself to actually thank

the man who'd just kicked Addie to the curb, Giff settled for a crisp nod, then strode from Bill's office.

Addie, I will fix this for you, I swear.

WITH TANNER AT SCHOOL and Nicole in daycare, Addie was huddled in her life-sucks/I-have-PMS flannel pajamas, trying to take advantage of this time alone and work through the worst of her grief and anger. She wanted to scream and sob the way Nicole did when she was too tired to sleep or when a new tooth was poking through the surface of her tender gums. Addie wanted to kick and flail. But ever since she'd driven out of that parking lot, Giff in her rearview mirror, her emotions had been frozen into an iceberg of pain just below the surface.

Nothing would come.

Addie was working on the theory that there were two key types of pain. There was the dull stab of trauma you saw coming but couldn't avoid—being downsized in company-wide layoffs, losing a relative who'd been sick for a while, breaking off a romantic relationship that both parties had quietly known for months wasn't working. And then there was the sharp, wrenching agony of the speeding train that came out of nowhere. Losing Zach and Diane. Losing her job.

Losing Giff.

Her fingers tightened convulsively on her cordless phone, and she tried once more to call Jonna. She got the voice mail for the second time and hung up. This was not the kind of thing you summarized in a message. *You know the great new guy in my life you encouraged me to date? He got me fired.*

Not that Addie for one second blamed Jonna for thinking Giff was great. They all had, even baby Nicole who giggled and cooed whenever she saw his face. Of course, baby Nicole had only been on the planet for a few months and didn't know about concepts like deception and betrayal. Addie didn't realize how hard she was squeezing the phone until the battery compartment fell off and clattered to the floor.

A sick, panicky feeling had gripped her, one she recognized from this summer in those first days after she'd brought Nicole and Tanner here. She'd felt so horribly isolated then, suffocating on fear. She'd just lost her big brother, who'd also been one of her closest friends; Christian had left her; Jonna had been largely unreachable as she explored a relationship that might well lead to getting married one day and marginalizing Addie's role in her life; and, perhaps worst of all, seeing how frail her own parents had been at Zach's funeral had forced her to admit that they were truly getting up there in years and that one day she would have to take care of arrangements for them the same way she had for her sibling.

It had been the bleakest time she'd ever known in her life and only in retrospect did she see how much Giff had helped her. Not just by the specific actions he'd taken but simply by *being* there. The moral support alone had calmed her enough to ease the paralyzing fright and allow her to be productive again. And now that had been yanked away, leaving her more alone and exposed than ever.

No, that's not true. You still have Jonna, she's just in a meeting right now or something. And Gabi's your friend. Assuming the woman didn't think Addie was a thief and refuse to ever speak to her again for fear of the association hurting Gabrielle's job.

"Hell with this," she said aloud. "I'll be my own moral support." If she didn't have a friend currently available to listen to her vent, then Addie could always self-medicate with Ben & Jerry.

Wait, no. They were *men.* Her lip curled as she recalled Bill Daughtrie's malicious glee in calling her into his office this morning without shutting the door. He'd made sure everyone in earshot knew exactly what was going on, and it had quickly spread to those who hadn't been close enough to catch every word for themselves.

For a moment, the dread tried to close in again— finding a good job in this economy was difficult enough without being blacklisted because people thought you were a corporate criminal. She shook it off; she'd worry about that part later. For now, forget Bill and Giff and even Ben & Jerry. Resolute, she marched into her kitchen with plans to raid her pantry and throw an all girl party with her friends Sara Lee and Betty Crocker. She thought there might be a Mrs. Smith's cobbler in the freezer.

She was preheating the oven when the knock came at the door. Her first, nonsensical thought was that Jonna had seen she'd called twice from the house phone and come straight over. But Jonna worked clear across town. Even if she'd reacted so strongly to a couple of missed calls, she couldn't have gotten here this fast.

Giff?

He'd certainly been persistent this morning in his attempts to talk to her. Too bad nothing he'd said had made the nightmare of her being fired any easier to accept. On the contrary, his garbled attempts at explanation had felt like getting stabbed in the same wound twice. Yet as another knock sounded her traitorous heart thudded in misguided anticipation. Had being happy to see him become such a Pavlovian response in the past few weeks? If it was Gifford Baker on the other side of that peephole, she was not opening the door.

"Who is it?" she called, walking from her kitchen to her living room.

"Pepper."

Addie felt her eyebrows shoot upward. Pepper was the last person in the world she'd expected on her doorstep. She recalled the woman's announcement just last week that she had Addie's back. At the time, Addie hadn't realized how much she might need that. *See, you're not alone.*

You just have very strange allies.

Addie swung her door open to find Pepper standing on the welcome mat with a white bakery bag, from which emanated the warm, comforting smell of chocolate chip cookies. And to Pepper's left, on the far end of Addie's porch, stood a tense-looking Giff, who emanated the stench of betrayal.

Addie's eyes snapped back to Pepper, furious.

"He's using me as a human shield," the other woman said derisively, "instead of manning up and coming here alone. This way there's a witness if you try to whack him. But you know me, Caine. I wouldn't have agreed to come along if I thought he was making a fool of either one of us. You should have heard him yelling at our boss after you left."

Addie wrapped her arms around herself. "*Your* boss." And she hadn't "left" so much as she'd been evicted from the building.

"Let us in," Pepper coaxed. She wiggled the white bag. "There are cookies in it for you."

Addie's eyes stung as she heard Giff's voice in her head. *There could be a giant pretzel in it for you.* She'd told him at the baseball game, "I'm not that easy." Oh, but she had been, hadn't she?

Pepper wasn't the type to ask for anything twice. Taking advantage of Addie's emotionally dazed state, she elbowed her way inside, Giff on her heels. "Let's hear what he has to say, and when he's done, if you feel like he should be whacked…well, I can be bought."

Both Giff and Addie swiveled to look at her in disbelief.

Her cheeks flushed ever so slightly and she looked chagrined for probably the first time in her entire adult life. "That was probably the wrong thing to say, given today's events."

"Probably." Giff finally spoke. "But in the interest of considering every possible angle, *can* you be bought?"

Pepper smirked. "Never say never, I suppose, not if the situation was right and the price was high enough. But I'm not stupid enough for something like this. Why on earth would I set up my own employer to fail? That's classic biting the hand that feeds you and lacks long-term planning skills. If the company folds from lost jobs or you get caught, you're out on the street. And you can't rely on whoever you're in bed with, figuratively speaking, to hire you because they'd already know you aren't trustworthy. I'm not your man."

"I believe you," Giff said, "but it may look suspicious to some that you picked this morning to quit."

Addie blinked. "You quit? Not because of what happened to me?"

The brunette shrugged. "I had other offers on the table. It's no secret that you and I are both qualified to be team leaders, yet had never been given a project. It's because we're women, and I'm not putting up with that crap anymore. Let Parnelli and Jenner and the others pick up our slack."

Emotionally drained, Addie wandered back to the couch, clearing off toys and books from one of the cushions so that Pepper would have a space to sit, too. Giff, she wanted as far away as possible.

He caught her gaze, trying to give her that earnest, you-can-trust-me look. She stared him down, not willing to be suckered by the same con twice.

"I know you aren't the guilty party," he said. "I told Bill last week you were being set up and he agreed not to pursue the issue until after this Friday. He promised he wouldn't bother you with this until I'd had more time to build my case—that this was clearly an attempt at misdirection. I was just as shocked by what happened this morn—" Probably realizing how asinine and inaccurate that statement sounded, he stopped himself. "Bill lied to me."

"Gosh." Addie widened her eyes. "Don't you hate it when people are dishonest?"

Pepper snickered, then sat on the sofa and opened

the bakery bag. She pulled out a cookie for herself and handed one to Addie. No cookie for Giff.

"I'm holding Bill to his original promise," Giff said. "I have until Friday. I'm going to find out who's really behind this."

"I appreciate you riding to my rescue," Addie said sardonically, "but don't you think it's a little late for that, Galahad?"

"Bill's going to have to fire the real culprit, and he's already lost Pepper. He'll be so short-handed by the end of the week that you can probably name your own salary and still get your job back. Hell, make him throw in corporate sponsorship for Tanner's soccer team if you want and get all the kids free uniforms. But even if you decide not to go back to work for Daughtrie—and who here could blame you?—we need to publicly clear your name. You don't want the specter of this hanging over you while you interview for new positions elsewhere."

Addie nibbled on the cookie, not really tasting it, and thought about what he'd said. He was right on all counts, which did nothing to lessen her anger with him.

"So I guess question number one," Giff asked, "is whether you've ever given anyone else in the department access to your password information?"

"Of course not," she said automatically.

"Not even in the case of a last-minute emergency? Maybe something had to be done immediately and they were having trouble logging into the system. You—"

"That is such a basic no-no that you're insulting my intelligence. And before you ask, no I don't have passcodes taped to the side of my desk or anything ridiculous like that, either."

The only risk-free way someone could have got her information was if they'd actually seen her... "Jenner," she breathed.

"Robert Jenner?" Giff asked, looking alert.

"This is just an observation," she said slowly, "it's hardly proof of his being a criminal mastermind."

"I think we can rule out any kind of mastermind," Pepper interjected.

"Right before you were brought on board, Giff, Jenner took a very *comforting* interest in me," she admitted. "He was always stopping by my desk, asking about the kids, bringing me tissues, hugging me. I remember him being perched on the corner of my desk on Zach's birthday. I was a mess that day, not thinking straight at all. It took me two tries to log-in correctly and I remember Jenner patting me on the shoulder."

"He did just buy that flashy new car," Pepper added. "Not to mention he accrued legal fees for a contentious divorce, is probably paying alimony through the nose and still seems to have enough left over to wine and dine a string of bimbos."

Giff's jaw had clenched in righteous indignation. He was obviously ticked about Robert Jenner trying to exploit Addie. He seemed to be conveniently overlooking that, because of his own career demands, he'd tried to do so, as well.

"This gives me a good starting point to really focus on," Giff said. "Addie, I can call and let you know what—"

"Just send me an e-mail to let me know how it all shakes out," she said, the thought of having a conversation with Giff too exhausting to contemplate. "I appreciate your standing up for me with Daughtrie after I left and I hope you figure out who's behind this whether it's Jenner or not, but I don't want to speak to you again."

He swallowed hard. "I know you're mad—you have every right to be—but you don't mean that."

She shot to her feet, unwilling to have her own feelings dictated to her. "The hell I don't. I—"

"And this is my cue to wait outside," Pepper said, slipping off the end of the couch and toward the door.

No one spoke again until she'd shut it behind her.

"You told me you loved me," Giff pointed out, the optimism in his expression nearly painful to see.

Was the man an idiot that he couldn't see how big a tactical mistake it was to bring up her declaration right now? As she recalled, he hadn't been able to say it back; now she wondered if she'd always been more emotionally invested.

"The very first time you ever asked me to lunch, that day we met Brooke in the bistro, why did you ask me to go with you?"

"I...wanted to get to know you better."

"Wanted to, or had been instructed to?"

He looked away, swearing savagely. "Both, all right? I discounted you as a possibility pretty early—"

"How early?"

"But Bill wanted me to pay special attention to you and Pepper since the two of you get paid less."

She stared at this man she'd honestly thought was the most trustworthy person she'd ever met. She hadn't even realized until now, when he was no longer standing beside her, how much she'd allowed herself to lean on him. It was like having a crutch ripped away from a crippled person.

"Get out of my apartment," she said softly. "I tried telling you before that I don't have time to date, and that's more true than ever. Not only do I have two kids to raise, I need to find a job."

"Keep in mind what I said. He might be willing to hire you back by the end of the week."

She shook her head, willing herself not to cry. "It doesn't matter what he wants, not anymore. I deserve a fresh start."

Chapter Sixteen

By two o'clock, the appeal of having some alone time to sort through her feelings had completely disappeared. Instead, Addie washed her face and called the elementary school to let them know she'd be picking Tanner up and not to put him on the day care van today. She'd thought it would be a nice treat for them—maybe they could go for ice cream. *No, forget that.* Her mind ricocheted away from the memory of slow dancing with Giff in a dark parking lot. Maybe she and her nephew could go see a matinee or something.

But she hadn't realized the unannounced change in schedule would alarm the little boy so much.

"Aunt Addie, what's wrong?" he asked, as the teacher on the sidewalk tried to help him into the car.

"Nothing, honey."

"But why are you here?"

"Get in, buddy, and we'll talk about it once you're buckled. We're holding up car pool." She felt terrible, the world's most self-absorbed mother figure, because for all of her initial hemming and hawing that she didn't want to date Giff because *Tanner* would be hurt if they broke up, this was the first time today the repercussions of telling Giff to go to hell were really dawning on her. *What am I going to tell the kid?*

She pulled away from the curb, trying to organize her thoughts as she exited the school parking lot.

"Aunt Addie, have you been crying?"

She refused to lie to him point-blank. "You know me, sweetie. I cry at everything. Remember?"

"Did someone die?" His voice trembled.

"What? Honey, no! Everyone is fine."

"Can we call Grandmom and Grandpop in Florida and make sure they're okay?" he asked, unconvinced.

"Sure, we can call them tonight if you want to," she said. "But everyone's all right. I do have some news, though. I'm not going to be working at my old job anymore."

"At the office I visited? With Gabi and the candy bars?" He sounded disappointed but no longer concerned that this was of life and death consequence.

"Right." She took a deep breath, bracing herself. "And Mr. Giff. He and I both worked there, but now I don't. And he won't be there much longer. He'll be moving on to another job. So we probably won't be seeing him anymore."

"But he didn't die?" Tanner clarified.

"No." *I resisted the urge to strangle him.* "I swear to you, no one died."

"We might see him sometimes, though, right?"

"I doubt it."

"But what if we ran into him at the grocery store? Or I saw him on TV at a baseball game?"

"I suppose either of those things could happen," she allowed.

"Will I still see Jonna?" he asked.

"Of course." She gave him a reassuring smile in the rearview mirror.

"But you don't work with her," he pointed out, trying to find the holes in Addie's logic.

Unable to continue with this particular line of questioning any longer, she asked brightly, "How about we go see a movie?"

"Okay. As long as there's no kissing."

Addie couldn't agree more.

To: Addie Caine
From: Giff Baker
Date: Thursday, September 30, 2010
Subject: You were right

Addie, how are you? I know you won't speak to me and am trying to respect your wishes but I did stoop to calling Jonna. Short of saying you'd set up some interviews she stonewalled me. I wanted to let you know that Robert Jenner was the person who sabotaged you, although he insists he would never have done so voluntarily. Once we had the slightest bit of proof to accuse him with, he turned on his partner, a woman in the finance department he'd been having an affair with. He claims the whole thing was originally her idea but that she didn't have the necessary e-skills and "seduced him" into cooperating on the first few jobs. He'd planned to take the pay off and quit but she blackmailed him into the Groverton bid.

If you've changed your mind about the fresh start, Daughtrie is desperate to have you back.

But not half as desperate as I am. I miss you. I'm sorry I hurt you. Mom and Jake and Brooke—people you would think would surround me with love and support now that I've had my heart handed to me—mostly call me names and suggest that I'm stupid for letting you go.
Giff

"ARE YOU SURE THERE'S NOT anything else I can do for you?" Jonna leaned against the kitchen counter Friday evening, looking miserable.

Addie glanced up from her kneeling position on the floor where she was tying Tanner's cleats before they left for the soccer field. "Jonna, you're loading my dishwasher. You helped me edit and copy résumés all week. You've let me cry on your shoulder, you brought me a bottle of wine last night, you even changed one of Nicole's big bomb diapers. You've gone above and beyond the call of best friend."

"I know, but..." Jonna pursed her lips, staring at Tanner. Neither woman was comfortable saying the *G* word in front of the little boy. "I feel guilty."

"Because you encouraged me to have a good time or because you're in a happy relationship? Because those are both ridiculous reasons to feel bad. I'll be fine." That's what she'd been telling herself since she tossed Giff out of the apartment Monday, but she'd missed him like crazy all week and yesterday's e-mail had only intensified the ache. "Now wish the Sea Turtles luck, and go enjoy your date with Sean."

"Okay." Jonna kissed Tanner's cheek, laughing when the boy put up the predictable fuss. "Go, Turtles! I know this week you guys can win for sure."

Tanner shrugged. "Mr. Giff says it's not about winning, it's about being a team."

The two women exchanged helpless glances. It wasn't as if Addie was going to forbid the boy to talk about his former friend. Even if it *did* feel as though she was being stabbed every time she heard his name.

"Mr. Giff is absolutely right," she said, standing. "Let's get your sister and hustle out to the soccer field so we have plenty of time to warm up."

In the car, Tanner said, "I know you said we won't be seeing Mr. Giff so much anymore, but he'll be at my game."

Her heart squeezed; she'd forgotten that Giff had promised to make the second game. "No, honey, I don't think he will." In his e-mail, he'd reiterated that he was respecting Addie's wishes. And she didn't want to be anywhere near him.

Did she?

Tanner was affronted. "Of course he will! He promised. Mr. Giff would never break a promise."

Since she and her nephew might disagree about that, she bit her tongue.

As they pulled onto the gravel lot adjacent to the fields, Tanner let out such a shriek that she almost drove into a tree.

"Tanner! Are you hurt? What was that?"

"No. Sorry," he added sheepishly. "But see? I *told* you. I told you Mr. Giff would be here! He promised me."

She ground her teeth together, not sure yet whether she was overjoyed that Giff hadn't let down the little boy or if she was irritated that he might consider using the kid to get to her.

"Well, go say a quick hello to him but then get your tush on the field. We've got a lot of practicing to do."

Addie dragged the sack of soccer balls to the field, along with water bottles for herself and Tanner. All the while she prided herself on never once looking toward Giff, but his being there was like an electric tingle over her spine. Goose bumps raised across her skin. He didn't approach her until right before the game, when Tanner had dragged Caleb off to the side for a man-to-man discussion of sportsmanship.

"I know you don't want to speak to me," Giff said, in lieu of a hello, "so you don't have to say a word. I won't bother you or Tanner again and I can let him know that I have work travel coming up. But I promised him I'd be here. I can barely live with having hurt you, I wasn't going to add hurting him to that."

Moved in spite of herself, Addie darted a glance at him, noting that his eyes were shadowed and bloodshot, his face leaner than it should have been. Had he lost weight this week? His jawline was also dusted with golden stubble. And his faded polo shirt, which sported an ink stain halfway down the side, was untucked. She'd never seen him so disheveled.

"You look like hell," she blurted.

His lips cracked in a wry grin. "Wish I could say the

same. At least then I could try to salvage my pride by telling myself you missed me."

"I…" Better to let it go. "Thank you for coming. Tanner would have been devastated if you weren't here."

He nodded, then turned toward his seat along the fence line.

Squeezing her eyes shut, she called after him, "I do miss you! I just don't… It's a trust thing." She tried to swallow past the lump in her throat, her voice cracking when she hollered, "Huddle up, Turtles!"

Addie hoped that, to anyone watching the game, it looked as if she was following along and not obsessing about her own love life. At random intervals, she'd loudly comment, "Nice effort, Turtles!" or "Good hustle." But the kids on the field could have been playing croquet for all she noticed.

She thought about her nephew's easy acceptance that Giff would be here and not let them down. Had he ever *really* let them down? There was the investigating her, but did she think that all FBI agents and undercover cops were bad people who should be punished for their jobs? And there was the painful humiliation of getting fired, but he'd fixed that so that she could come back if she wanted. Frankly, she was pretty excited about one of the job interviews she'd lined up for next week, so returning to Daughtrie looked like a distant Plan B.

Addie was angry that he'd slept with her all the while knowing her job might be in danger, but men tended to compartmentalize their professional and personal lives more than women. Was being angry a good enough reason to throw away one of the best things that had ever happened to her? She bit her lip, jumping guiltily when the other coach announced that it was halftime.

Tanner jogged off the field, sweaty but happy. "Did you see that, Aunt Addie? I was *this close* to making the goal."

Guiltily, she promised herself she'd pay better attention once the game resumed. And she was certainly glad she did—instead of hogging the ball, which they'd discussed at every practice so far, Caleb passed it to Tanner who scored in the last quarter, putting the Sea Turtles ahead by one. Addie cheered like a maniac, congratulating both boys.

"Great goal, Tanner! Great teamwork, Caleb!" Without even thinking about it, she turned reflexively to find Giff, sharing the moment with him. He held his thumb up, grinning like a proud papa bear.

Whether the Turtles held on to their slight lead or not for the few remaining minutes of the game, this one had been close and they could hold their heads high. It in no way resembled last week's fiasco. Crying Sam hadn't even shed a single tear! One of the kids on the other team attempted a desperate high kick even though he was on completely the opposite side of the field from his goal, and several of the Turtles scrambled to get control of the ball. Tanner sprinted toward it, misjudging where it would land, and got nailed squarely in the head, falling backward.

"Tanner!" Trying not to think about the memo she'd seen about freak brain injuries being the reason this league didn't allow head shots, she raced toward Tanner. It wasn't until she reached his side that she realized Giff was right next to her, somehow having caught up even though he'd been farther away.

Tanner glanced up at the two of them and frowned. "Could someone help me up?"

"You sure you're all right?" Addie demanded, checking him for bruises or cuts. "How many fingers am I holding up?"

"Two. Jeesh. I'm fine. Tell her, Mr. Giff."

"You go sit with Giff, I'm calling in a substitution." Addie felt foolish for overreacting, shaky in the aftermath of her adrenaline rush. Mandy filled in for Tanner and acquitted herself well but no one else scored. Tanner had made the last goal of the game, taking the Turtles to victory.

"I'm proud of you," Giff was telling the boy when Addie walked over, having said goodbye to the last of her team parents. "I saw you working with Caleb over on the side earlier. I know he's not always the nicest kid in the world, but you reached out to him."

"He's my teammate," Tanner said self-importantly.

Giff laughed, then met Addie's gaze. "Well, sport, I think everything's done here. I should let you guys get home so you can jump in the tub. No offense, but you stink."

Tanner didn't appear to be listening. "Mr. Giff, Aunt Addie says we won't be seeing you much anymore."

"Well, I'll be busy with work," he hedged.

"You told me you weren't too busy for me," Tanner rebutted. "At the Astros game."

Addie sighed. Her nephew had a memory like an elephant.

"It's complicated," Giff said, shooting Addie

questioning glances as if asking her how he should handle this.

"Is it my fault?" Tanner asked. "Because I don't like kissing?"

"What? No," Addie assured him. Antsy for something to do besides stare at Giff, she pulled Nicole out of her stroller to check the baby's diaper before they piled into the car.

"Because you two haven't kissed each other since we got here."

Giff squatted down, looking Tanner straight in the eye. "You want the truth, sport? I did something that wasn't very nice to your aunt, kind of like breaking a promise. And she doesn't want to kiss me anymore."

"Oh." Tanner's face fell. "Did you say you're sorry? People should apologize if they're mean."

"He said he was sorry," Addie affirmed, not wanting Giff to paint himself as too much the bad guy. She'd told him earlier that she wasn't sure she trusted him but when something good had happened, she'd automatically turned to him. More telling, when something bad had happened, he'd automatically been right beside her, holding her hand.

"Well, did you forgive him?" Tanner demanded. "That's what teammates should do."

Teammates. The term bemused her. Was that how Tanner saw them, not as a family, exactly—she didn't want him to think anyone was replacing his parents—but as a team: himself, her, Mr. Giff and baby Nicole? A team that pulled together to support each other and had fun together and sometimes suffered losses but ultimately prevailed.

"Do you think you could forgive me, Coach?" Giff's tone was hoarse. "I know I fumbled, and you have every right to bench me, but, before you make your final decision, I want you to know...I love you, Addie."

Tears sprang to her eyes. "I love you, too." The words welled up in her naturally, with no hesitation. Even though she was angry, her feelings hadn't changed. "And I forgive you."

At first Giff's face went blank, as if he couldn't believe what he'd just heard but then he grabbed her, spinning her around with a shout of joy.

On the ground beside them, Tanner giggled. "Cover your eyes, Nicole, there's going to be more kissing."

Epilogue

"How was practice?" Addie Baker asked, as her husband walked into their spacious living room, holding Nicole in one arm and a soccer ball in the other. Through the floor-to-window ceiling behind him, the Texas sun was setting in fiery pink and orange streaks.

Giff's handsome face lit in the same smile of welcome he'd been giving her since the day she walked down the aisle to him. "Pretty good. Tanner's excited about being goalie on Saturday." He put down Nicole so that the toddler could scramble over to where Addie sat on the sectional sofa, gleefully shrieking, "Mama!"

Addie glanced past Giff in question. "So where is Tanner?"

"Kitchen. He said he was starving—even lifted up his shirt so I could see his protruding ribs."

She laughed. "Yeah, it's amazing he hasn't wasted away on what little we feed him."

"Enough about all of us, though. How are you?" Giff's green eyes filled with gentle concern. "Feeling any better? I was surprised when you called me today and asked me to take over practice. You've never missed one, Coach."

"I'm going to be fine." Happiness swelled in her, so full that tears threatened to squeeze out, as if her body simply couldn't hold in that much emotion. "Although I did call and make a doctor's appointment for tomorrow."

"You think it's that stomach bug going around the preschool?"

"Potty!" Nicole suddenly declared.

Giff scooped up their little girl, getting her to the nearest restroom in record speed. He returned soon after, shaking his head. "False alarm, but at least she's showing an interest. Mark my words, diapers will be out of our lives very soon."

Addie let out a peal of laughter. "Maybe not as soon as you think. You know how I keep trying to talk you into hiring Pepper to join us?" Last year, Addie had quit her job in favor of helping Giff expand his consulting business.

At the mention of Pepper, he made his usual face of affected horror.

"Come on," Addie scoffed, "she's not that bad. You just have to get to know her better. Besides, you might need her. You're going to be shorthanded when I go on maternity leave, Mr. Baker."

His eyes widened, then flew to her midsection as if he could somehow discern the new life blossoming there. She'd been suspicious for the past couple of days and had taken two tests while the rest of her family was at the soccer field. Getting the doctor's confirmation tomorrow was a formality. Then they could share the news with Grace, who was already a fantastic grandmother, and their closest friends.

"You're… We're…?"

She nodded, too choked up for words. Tears dripped freely down her cheeks. When she'd pulled herself together enough to speak again, she asked, "How do you feel about adding another player to the family roster?"

He cupped her face with his hands, leaning in for a soft kiss. "Go team."

* * * * *

HARLEQUIN®

COMING NEXT MONTH

Available October 12, 2010

#1325 THE TRIPLETS' FIRST THANKSGIVING
Babies & Bachelors USA
Cathy Gillen Thacker

#1326 ELLY: COWGIRL BRIDE
The Codys: The First Family of Rodeo
Trish Milburn

#1327 THE RELUCTANT WRANGLER
Roxann Delaney

#1328 FAMILY MATTERS
Barbara White Daille

REQUEST YOUR FREE BOOKS!
2 FREE NOVELS PLUS 2 FREE GIFTS!

HARLEQUIN®

American ★ Romance®

Love, Home & Happiness!

YES! Please send me 2 FREE Harlequin® American Romance® novels and my 2 FREE gifts (gifts are worth about $10). After receiving them, if I don't wish to receive any more books, I can return the shipping statement marked "cancel." If I don't cancel, I will receive 4 brand-new novels every month and be billed just $4.24 per book in the U.S. or $4.99 per book in Canada. That's a saving of at least 15% off the cover price! It's quite a bargain! Shipping and handling is just 50¢ per book.* I understand that accepting the 2 free books and gifts places me under no obligation to buy anything. I can always return a shipment and cancel at any time. Even if I never buy another book from Harlequin, the two free books and gifts are mine to keep forever.

154/354 HDN E5LG

Name	(PLEASE PRINT)

Address	Apt. #

City	State/Prov.	Zip/Postal Code

Signature (if under 18, a parent or guardian must sign)

Mail to the **Harlequin Reader Service:**
IN U.S.A.: P.O. Box 1867, Buffalo, NY 14240-1867
IN CANADA: P.O. Box 609, Fort Erie, Ontario L2A 5X3

Not valid for current subscribers to Harlequin® American Romance® books.

Want to try two free books from another line?
Call 1-800-873-8635 or visit www.morefreebooks.com.

* Terms and prices subject to change without notice. Prices do not include applicable taxes. N.Y. residents add applicable sales tax. Canadian residents will be charged applicable provincial taxes and GST. Offer not valid in Quebec. This offer is limited to one order per household. All orders subject to approval. Credit or debit balances in a customer's account(s) may be offset by any other outstanding balance owed by or to the customer. Please allow 4 to 6 weeks for delivery. Offer available while quantities last.

Your Privacy: Harlequin is committed to protecting your privacy. Our Privacy Policy is available online at www.eHarlequin.com or upon request from the Reader Service. From time to time we make our lists of customers available to reputable third parties who may have a product or service of interest to you. If you would prefer we not share your name and address, please check here. ☐

Help us get it right—We strive for accurate, respectful and relevant communications. To clarify or modify your communication preferences, visit us at www.ReaderService.com/consumerschoice.

HAR10R

HARLEQUIN®

A *Romance*

FOR EVERY MOOD™

Spotlight on

Inspirational

Wholesome romances
that touch the heart and soul.

See the next page
to enjoy a sneak peek from
the Love Inspired® inspirational series.

*See below for a sneak peek at
our inspirational line, Love Inspired®.
Introducing HIS HOLIDAY BRIDE
by bestselling author Jillian Hart*

Autumn Granger gave her horse rein to slide toward the town's new sheriff.

"Hey, there." The man in a brand-new Stetson, black T-shirt, jeans and riding boots held up a hand in greeting. He stepped away from his four-wheel drive with "Sheriff" in black on the doors and waded through the grasses. "I'm new around here."

"I'm Autumn Granger."

"Nice to meet you, Miss Granger. I'm Ford Sherman, from Chicago." He knuckled back his hat, revealing the most handsome face she'd ever seen. Big blue eyes contrasted with his sun-tanned complexion.

"I'm guessing you haven't seen much open land. Out here, you've got to keep an eye on cows or they're going to tear your vehicle apart."

"What?" He whipped around. Sure enough, mammoth black-and-white creatures had started to gnaw on his four-wheel drive. They clustered like a mob, mouths and tongues and teeth bent on destruction. One cow tried to pry the wiper off the windshield, another chewed on the side mirror. Several leaned through the open window, licking the seats.

"Move along, little dogie." He didn't know the first thing about cattle.

The entire herd swiveled their heads to study him curiously. Not a single hoof shifted. The animals soon returned to chewing, licking, digging through his possessions.

Autumn laughed, a warm and wonderful sound. "Thanks,

I needed that." She then pulled a bag from behind her saddle and waved it at the cows. "Look what I have, guys. Cookies."

Cows swung in her direction, and dozens of liquid brown eyes brightened with cookie hopes. As she circled the car, the cattle bounded after her. The earth shook with the force of their powerful hooves.

"Next time, you're on your own, city boy." She tipped her hat. The cowgirl stayed on his mind, the sweetest thing he had ever seen.

Will Ford be able to stick it out in the country
to find out more about Autumn?
Find out in HIS HOLIDAY BRIDE
by bestselling author Jillian Hart,
available in October 2010
only from Love Inspired®.

FROM #1 *NEW YORK TIMES*
AND *USA TODAY* BESTSELLING AUTHOR

DEBBIE MACOMBER

Mrs. Miracle on 34th Street...

This Christmas, Emily Merkle (just call her Mrs. Miracle) is working in the toy department at Finley's, the last family-owned department store in Manhattan.

Her boss (who happens to be the owner's son) has placed an order for a large number of high-priced robots, which he hopes will give the business a much-needed boost. In fact, Jake Finley's counting on it.

Holly Larson is counting on that robot, too. She's been looking after her eight-year-old nephew, Gabe, ever since her widowed brother was deployed overseas. Holly plans to buy Gabe a robot—which she can't afford—because she's determined to make Christmas special.

But this Christmas will be different—thanks to Mrs. Miracle. Next to bringing children joy, her favorite activity is giving romance a nudge. Fortunately, Jake and Holly are receptive to her "hints." And thanks to Mrs. Miracle, Christmas takes on new meaning for Jake. For all of them!

Call Me Mrs. Miracle

**Available wherever books are sold
September 28!**